My First Love

Don't miss any of the books in **Love Stories** – a terrific new series of romances from Bantam Books:

Love Stories

My First Love

CALLIE WEST

BANTAM BOOKS
TORONTO • NEW YORK • LONDON • SYDNEY • AUCKLAND

LOVE STORIES: MY FIRST LOVE
A BANTAM BOOK : 0 553 40976 X

First publication in Great Britain

PRINTING HISTORY
Bantam Press edition published 1997

Bantam Books are published by Transworld Publishers Ltd,
61–63 Uxbridge Road, Ealing, London W5 5SA,
in Australia by Transworld Publishers (Australia) Pty Ltd,
15–25 Helles Avenue, Moorebank, NSW 2170,
and in New Zealand by Transworld Publishers (NZ) Ltd,
3 William Pickering Drive, Albany, Auckland.

Printed and bound in Great Britain by
Cox & Wyman Ltd, Reading, Berkshire.

To Elizabeth

My First Love

Chapter One

T HE NIGHT RICK Finnegan kissed me changed my life—but not in the way I'd expected.

He had given me a ride home from my best friend Blythe Carlson's house, where we'd all been drilling one another on vocabulary for the PSATs. There we were, sitting in his dad's Buick outside the Palms bungalow apartments, where my mom and I live, when out of nowhere Rick slipped his arm around me.

I don't know what got into him, but one minute he'd been defining the word *alacrity*, and the next thing I knew he was demonstrating it. He moved across the seat so fast that I didn't have time to react. Suddenly, his mouth was on mine. Instinctively, I closed my eyes—and he kissed me.

"Amy, I . . . I think I'm starting to like you," Rick whispered.

My eyes flew open in surprise. But instead of seeing Rick, I saw Chris Shepherd, who's on my swim team, the Dolphins, and in my physics class, too. He's also the guy I've been daydreaming about for weeks. "I'm the one you really want," Chris-in-my-mind said. I gasped and jumped away from Rick, leaving him to kiss air where my face had been.

"Rick!" I shrieked, staring at him.

"Amy?" Rick said, looking sheepish. "Are you mad? What's wrong?"

"N-n-nothing," I stuttered, trying to collect my thoughts. I couldn't believe that Rick Finnegan—my buddy since kindergarten—had just kissed me!

I put my hand on his shoulder. "Look, Rick," I said gently, "I'm very flattered. You're a great guy. But we're friends—and I'd like to keep it at that. I've got so much going on right now, I don't have time for romance."

But Rick didn't look convinced. "Amy," he said, twisting a lock of my straight blond hair around his finger, "you know what they say about all work and no play. . . ."

"Maybe," I said, stepping out of the car, "but all play and no work gets you a career dipping cones at the Dairy Queen."

Actually, I didn't say that. I didn't even think up this perfect comeback until the next day. What came out instead were my mother's words, words often meant for me.

"Your passion is misguided," I informed him, closing the car door behind me.

"My *what*?" I saw Rick's lips form the question behind the window glass right before I waved and turned away.

I couldn't believe I had said that. Mom uses *passion* in a way that doesn't have anything to do with kissing. It has to do with enthusiasm and ambition.

According to my mom, passion, like money, runs out. So you have to be careful not to spend it carelessly. My father, for example, turned out to be a bad investment. He wasn't around long enough to see me turn two. I don't really remember him, but Mom said that once she'd loved him so much her heart hurt. After he took off, she poured what was left of her passion into me.

"Don't throw away your talents the way I did," my mom was always warning me. Believe me, I wasn't planning to, not when my whole future, starting with a swimming scholarship to college, was at stake.

I felt kind of bad saying what I did to Rick, but I guess the kiss really caught me off guard. I turned again to go back and apologize, but he was already driving away.

I stood for a minute outside our apartment, looking up at the stars and thinking about the fact that one of my oldest and best friends just kissed me. When did Rick's feelings for me change, and why hadn't I realized it? I had felt nothing when Rick's lips were on mine. But for some unknown reason just the thought of Chris Shepherd's lips sent my heart racing. It was true what I'd said to Rick. I never *had* had time for guys. Until now.

Chris and I had known each other for a couple of years from the swim team, but he had never treated me any differently from the way he had treated any other girl on the Dolphins. He was always friendly, and he kidded around, but that was it.

I had always liked Chris, but over the last few months I had been noticing different things about him—admiring his long, lean body, his thick, glossy brown hair, his quick sense of humor . . .

I shook my head to get rid of the thoughts. I had feelings for Chris I'd never had before for a guy, but I was still too shy to do anything about it. He had been a fantasy tonight, and he'd probably always be a fantasy, I thought dejectedly as I headed inside our apartment.

"You're just in time for the latest episode of *Search for the Stars*," Mom said as I walked into

4

our combination living/dining room. Mom worked two jobs. She worked from nine to three at the Arizona Bank, and evenings at El Rancho supermarket. Every day she taped her favorite soaps, and when she got home from the El Rancho, she'd curl up on the couch and watch them.

"Thanks, but I've been studying vocabulary for hours," I told her. "I'm afraid I'll erase what I've learned if I zone out on TV."

"Good for you," Mom said. "You go ahead and get a good night's sleep."

"I think I will." I hesitated for a moment. "Mom? Something pretty weird just happened," I said.

"What?"

"Well . . . Rick drove me home from Blythe's. And . . . he . . . well, he, um . . . told me he liked me," I explained, blushing. I didn't think I needed to tell her about the kiss. It was kind of embarrassing.

Mom sat up straight. "What did you say?"

"I told him I didn't like him that way. That we were just friends." I watched as Mom breathed an almost undetectable sigh of relief.

"Good answer, honey. With your schedule, a boyfriend is the last thing you need," she said.

"Yeah. I guess," I said, shrugging.

I kissed her on the cheek and went to my room. There's no way I could have sat through the soap. I was having a hard enough time already putting Chris out of my mind and concentrating on my work. The last thing I needed at the moment was to fill my aching brain with stories about star-crossed lovers and abandoned dreams.

The PSAT, it turned out, was a nightmare of words I'd never used and math I'd understood for about an hour in ninth grade. It was bad enough that my brain was fried from choosing among A, B, C, or none of the above and that my hand was numb from filling in those tiny circles with a sweat-slick number-two pencil. But the worst part was the reel-to-reel reruns of that kiss that played in my head all day.

And it wasn't Rick's kiss that I kept seeing—that was something we'd both like to forget, I was sure. It was Chris's. I couldn't stop picturing what it would be like to kiss him. In my mind his lips were soft and warm and firm. Then, when his lips found mine, I had that roller-coaster feeling—my heart plunged into my stomach and then began the slow, suspenseful crawl right back up to my chest.

The next thing I knew, I was sighing so loudly that people on both sides of me turned and stared. At the same time the proctor announced, "Fifteen minutes left." What was I *doing*? How could I blow this? Embarrassed and frantic, I raced through the rest of the test.

6

*　　*　　*

I was relieved when the PSATs were over, though considering my state of mind when I'd taken it, I was worried about my score. As we left the room, everyone seemed to be talking at once.

"Did you finish the analogy section?"

"How do you find the least common denominator in fractions?"

"Does anyone know what *apposite* means?"

For the rest of the day my honors classes were a chorus of collective anxiety. When my last class was over, at three o'clock, I fled to the gym, where I hoped to somehow rinse myself of it all by putting on my racing suit and plunging into the pool before practice.

The rest of the team wasn't due to help put in the lanes for another half hour, so I had the open pool to myself. I love swimming more than anything else in the world. As I stood on the deck and looked at the tranquil water, I began to feel calm. For the next two hours, all I'd have to do was concentrate on picking up another win in the 100 free-style this weekend.

I took a few running steps and blasted the water's smooth surface with a cannonball. As always, the water was chilly, so I started swimming warm-ups, steaming back and forth from end to end. Believe me, after two seasons on the swim team, I knew that pool so well that I could swim it in my sleep.

By the fourth lap I was cruising—when suddenly I crashed into someone and swallowed a mouthful of water.

"Amy, are you all right?" asked a soft male voice as I surfaced, coughing. It was Chris. He grabbed my hand to steady me, which to my embarrassment landed smack in the middle of his chest.

"I'm fine," I said, coughing again. I wiped the water dribbling from my mouth off my chin. "I didn't see you."

"I'm sorry," he said. "I saw you swimming laps when I got into the water. I should have gotten out of your way. I know it sounds stupid, but I was just floating on my back and thinking." He looked at me with real concern. "I'm sorry."

"Don't sweat it," I said shyly. "It's just that I thought I had the pool to myself." I wanted to duck my whole face underwater or at least hide my eyes. Could he tell by looking, I wondered, that my mind was spinning constant reruns about kissing him?

Chris returned to floating on his back. His brown hair fanned out like a paintbrush behind him. "If you close your eyes," he said, "you can pretend it's a lake, it's so calm and quiet."

I watched him as he lazily kicked his legs and drifted, eyes closed, toward the middle of the pool. "What are you doing?" I asked.

"I'm watching myself break the regional record for the breaststroke," he explained.

Great, I thought. *While I'm picturing kisses, he's imagining fame.* Nervously, I asked, "Do you really think imagining something can make it come true?"

Chris laughed. "I'll know when I reach the finish line."

Even though he looked sort of strange floating there, I admired his quiet determination. Chris is the fastest swimmer on the Dolphins, but breaking the breaststroke record was something that he had never been able to do.

I loved watching him. His body was long and thin, yet muscular, and he moved as though he felt completely comfortable in it. I'm about 5' 7" and pretty thin myself, but I don't move as gracefully as Chris. Before I started swimming with the Dolphins my freshman year, I was really skinny. Now I wore my muscles carefully, like a rental I'd have to return when swim season was over.

Several Dolphins came into the pool area, their voices sending echoes across the floor tiles. Not even this commotion disturbed Chris's concentration. I wondered what part of the race he was mentally swimming just then.

As he drifted nearby, I wanted to reach down

9

and gently stir the water, send it rippling to touch him. Instead, I ducked my head back under and continued swimming laps.

I swam freestyle for a few lengths, feeling confident in the water—until I made a graceless flip turn, whacking my heel against the lip of the pool.

"Ouch!" I yelled. I hadn't meant to draw attention to myself, but as I limped along the bottom of the pool to the starting blocks, I could see that Chris was moving toward my lane. My heart skipped a beat when I realized he was waiting for me.

"Your timing's off," he told me when I stopped to get my breath. He touched my wrist and I was suddenly aware of his long, strong fingers. I stiffened, and he must have noticed, because he took his hand away immediately and let it skim the surface of the pool.

"That's what Coach August says," I said, trying to sound casual, as though my wrist weren't burning from his touch. "He says I turn too late."

"Not too late, exactly, but too cautiously. Your turn would be right on target if you didn't mentally pull back just as you get to the wall. It's like you trip yourself up."

Chris was probably right—it wasn't so much the turn as it was the dread of it that kept me from swimming full speed. I constantly imagined bashing my heels. And that was exactly what kept happening.

"You could do a neater flip turn and probably shave twenty seconds off your time if you didn't hold back but just charged," Chris said. "Otherwise, it's like you're swimming with your mental brakes on."

"That makes sense," I said. "But how do I charge if I'm terrified I'll hit the lip of the pool?"

"By picturing doing it perfectly so many times that you really believe you can." He waded over to grab a kickboard from the pool deck. "First," he said, tossing me the Styrofoam board, "you've got to relax. Here, float and breathe deeply." He walked over and steadied the board.

But it was hard to relax with Chris staring down at me. I lay there looking up at him. All I could think about were his deep-set brown eyes. There was an intensity in them, and a kindness as well. I felt like I was about to blush.

"Good so far," Chris said, gently brushing his fingers across my brow. He had these hands that looked honest—slim fingers, one wrist tied with a frayed leather friendship bracelet. "Now, close your eyes."

I squeezed them shut and waited. "Not so tight," Chris advised. "What do you see?"

You, I wanted to say. Aloud I said, "I see myself

11

lying on a kickboard, looking stupid, in the middle of the pool."

"Amy, be serious."

"I am." At first, I was too self-conscious to imagine anything but the rest of the Dolphins making fun of me. But after a while, I got the hang of it. I saw myself in the practice pool, speeding toward the end of the lane. I was surprised that the mental picture was so vivid. "I'm swimming," I said, still feeling kind of silly.

"And?"

"I'm watching the lane lines, getting close to the lip."

"Okay, now try to imagine keeping up your speed. What are you thinking?"

"Don't hit the lip, don't hit it, don't hit it— wham!" I opened my eyes then, and instinctively reached down to rub my heel.

"Try again," Chris said gently.

"What's the use?" I moaned. "It's like a movie someone else is directing." Sometimes my whole life felt like that.

I thought then that he'd give up, but instead he urged me on. "This time, instead of thinking 'Don't hit it,' try thinking 'Flip.'"

I closed my eyes and was mentally halfway down the lane when I stopped midstroke to ask, "Why?"

"Because your brain takes the 'don't' out of

'don't hit the lip.' And your body only does what your brain tells it to."

If that was true, I was in trouble, because there were plenty of my mother's "don'ts" rattling around in my head. *Don't apologize for your intelligence, don't mope about what you don't have, don't take your education for granted, don't underestimate yourself, don't expect something for nothing, don't throw away your future on some guy.* For years I'd been repeating those commands in my head, maybe dooming myself to do the very things I'd told myself not to do.

In my mind, I began my stroke again, saying, "Flip, flip, flip," under my breath, swimming as fast as I could imagine. Then, before I knew it, I'd turned in the water almost effortlessly.

"Hey, I did it!" I said, and opened my eyes in time to see Chris looking at me intently, studying me the way I'd studied him.

Just then Coach August blew his whistle, signaling it was time to put the lanes in for practice. I slid off the kickboard and let myself sink. "Thanks," I said shyly.

"Anytime," Chris said, smiling. Then he turned away and swam toward the coach.

Anytime, I thought happily as I dove underwater.

Anytime . . .

★   ★   ★

I was the last one to leave the girls' locker room after practice that afternoon, mostly because I was thinking so much about Chris that I couldn't get moving. As I walked out of school, he was sitting in the grass by my bus stop.

I was surprised. He lived on the east side of town, and I lived on the west. "Hey, Chris," I called out as I crossed the street, "aren't you waiting for the wrong bus?"

"I was waiting for you," he said.

I thought my heart would stop. "Me?" I managed to say.

He smiled as he stood up and brushed the grass off his faded, torn Levi's. "Yeah," he said. "I thought you might want a ride home."

"You've got a car?"

He pointed in the direction of the school parking lot behind me. "It's my brother Dave's. It's that sixty-four Mustang," he said. "Dave said I could use it today. He's home on break from college."

I turned and saw this gleaming, classic car. I knew that Chris came from a pretty wealthy family, but because he always wore Levi's with holes in the knees, T-shirts, and baseball caps, I never thought about it. "Cool," I said as we walked toward the convertible, trying to conceal the excitement I felt.

Chris opened the car door, and I got in. As he

slipped into the driver's side, I glanced at him out of the corner of my eye. Just the night before, I had been in Rick's car, being kissed by him and seeing Chris. Now I was actually in a car with Chris! Maybe thinking about things really could make them happen.

Chapter Two

"**D**O YOU WANT to celebrate something with me?" Chris asked as he turned onto Central Avenue.

"What are you celebrating?" I asked, willing the nervousness out of my voice.

Chris grinned at me as he pulled up to a stoplight. "I'm celebrating the occasion of driving you home."

"If that's your idea of a party, you ought to get out more," I said. I was trying to sound witty and nonchalant, but I could feel my heart pounding in my chest.

"I would, if I had a good reason . . . if I had the right girl."

Suddenly I felt so shy I didn't know what to do or say. In my rush to fill the silence between us, I said something really dumb.

"So," I said lamely, "I hear you scored over fifteen hundred on your SATs."

Chris winced. "Who told you my scores?"

"No one in particular—I mean, it's all over school."

"Don't people have anything more interesting to gossip about?"

"That's pretty interesting to me," I said defensively. "I've never known anyone who scored that high. Why wouldn't you want people to know?"

"Because it doesn't mean anything," he said.

"Of course it does. I'd kill for a score like that." I laughed. "You can't tell me scores don't matter. The college counselor told me I'd be in the running for a merit scholarship if I get a high score on the PSAT."

"But what I'm saying is that it doesn't matter in the larger scheme of things."

"How large a scheme are we talking here?" I asked. "To me, getting into a good school is a pretty big deal."

"It is for me too!" The light turned green, and Chris hit the accelerator so suddenly, I was pinned for a second against my seat. He put out his arm to steady me. "Sorry," he said. "It's just that I'm sick of how every junior and senior I know can't talk about anything but college, as though that's the only reason we get out of bed in the morning."

"I know what you mean," I told Chris. "But I can't help worrying about grades and SATs. I'm going to need a good financial aid package for college—it's just me and my mom at home. So I feel a lot of pressure to get good grades. Like in physics, for instance. I hate that class. Sometimes I just want to throw the stupid book right across the room."

"We could study together," Chris suggested. "I could use some help with physics too."

"Oh, right," I couldn't help saying. He was one of the best students in the class.

"I'm serious," he said, his face turning red. "Right now, class seems pretty dull. It might be different if I had a . . ."

He turned to me, and his voice trailed off.

"What?" I asked.

Chris shook his head, as if to clear it. "If only I had a teacher this year who had some *fire*. But it's like Mr. Tayerle's teaching in his sleep, re-using old lesson plans from 1955."

I laughed. "I've seen his notes up close," I said. "The pages are so old, they're curled up on the edges and yellow."

"Exactly." Chris laughed too. "You do know what I mean."

At Glendale Avenue, Chris was supposed to turn right to get to my apartment, like I'd told him, but instead he pulled into the left lane and stopped for the light. "Detour?" he asked me. "There's something out here that you just have to see."

A feeling of worry skidded around my stomach as I looked at my watch. As I thought of my mom getting ready to leave the bank for her shift at the supermarket, her favorite word—*passion*—popped into my head again.

Passion was the thing that kept me up late to memorize a phone-book-sized vocabulary list, and to spend hours revising to turn a *B* English paper into an *A*. It was the thing that made me dive into the chilly practice pool day after day.

Was it passion that made my heart thump when Chris's knee grazed mine? And was that passion the misguided variety?

I looked up and saw Chris gazing at me expectantly. "Um, okay," I heard my voice say, though my brain was politely telling him I had to get home.

I leaned back into the seat cushions as the Mustang picked up speed. "It won't take too long, though, will it?" I managed to ask. "I've got about four hours of homework waiting for me." As I spoke, I suddenly had this nagging feeling that there was somewhere else I was supposed to be, something else I was supposed to be doing.

I guess I must have been frowning, because Chris said, "Don't worry so much, Amy. This will be worth it, I promise. And I'll even get you home before dark."

He was right. Of course he was. *Get a grip, Amy,* I ordered myself. I was going for a drive, not eloping. I was entitled to go out with a guy once in a while. My GPA wasn't going to plummet just because I was having fun.

So I stopped worrying, and I let myself enjoy the open feeling in the convertible—the way the wind pulled my skin tight as it rushed against my face. I had to admit I also liked seeing other people's envious expressions, shut up inside their cars with their air conditioners blasting while our hair blew free.

It was almost six o'clock, and it was still really warm for October. But the sun was sinking. My hair was still wet, and I began to shiver. I started searching through my gym bag for my sweatshirt. I must have left it in my locker, though, because all I came up with was a bathing cap, a candy bar, and five different-colored socks.

"Are you cold?" Chris asked when he saw me wearing two of the socks as mittens.

"Not really," I said, plucking the sock-mittens off. I didn't want him to think I was some tender flower. I'm not. It's just that I've lived my whole life in Arizona, and my blood's like a lizard's—it needs direct sun to stay warm. "I was just trying to find my Dolphins sweatshirt."

"Here, take the wheel," he said. He reached into the backseat for his gym bag.

"Hey!" I cried, grabbing the wheel. In my moment of panic at having to take over the driving, I almost steered us right out of the lane.

Unfazed, Chris kept groping around in the backseat. "My sweatshirt's in here somewhere," he muttered. Finally, he snagged his athletic bag and tossed it into my lap. Then, when he went to take the steering wheel again, his hands landed on top of mine. They were so warm. I swallowed hard.

"Can you get it?" he asked.

"Uh, sure, thank you," I said, sliding my freezing fingers out from under his.

"No problem," Chris said.

Given the way he dressed, I didn't expect the inside of Chris's gym bag to be neat. It wasn't. I pushed aside damp swim trunks, empty cola cans, pencils, balled-up notebook paper, and a dog-eared copy of *The Catcher in the Rye* before I spotted the beady eye of our Dolphin mascot.

I tugged at the neck of the sweatshirt, trying to free it from the rest of the rubble. As I did, a spiral notebook fell into my lap. I swear I wasn't snooping—it opened right up to a page bookmarked with an ice cream bar wrapper.

And there on that page was my name. Amy Wyse. Written not just once but over and over in a hundred different styles.

My heart stopped. My breath caught in my

22

throat. I could practically hear the blood rushing to my face.

"Did you find it?" Chris asked.

"No! What, the sweatshirt? Y-y-yes!" I stammered, closing the notebook quickly and stuffing it back into the bag.

My heart soared as I pictured the notebook again in my mind. It was wonderful. It was incredible. Chris liked me. Why hadn't I seen it before?

Just then something strange happened. It's hard to explain, but I felt like my heart opened up a little bit to let some new and strange feelings in.

And I had the scary feeling it might be hard to close it again.

"You look good in that," Chris said, as if he'd never seen me in Dolphin duds before, as if our sweatshirts weren't exactly alike. "The blue lettering matches your eyes exactly."

"Thanks," I said, feeling sheepish. Once I finally had the sweatshirt on, I found I didn't need it after all. Maybe I'd gotten used to the wind—or maybe seeing my name written over and over in Chris's notebook was what had made me feel so warm. But I didn't want to take it off either. It smelled faintly of chlorine, just the way all my swimming clothes did. But beneath that, there was another, sweet smell—lotion? shampoo?—

that was familiar and pleasant. I couldn't quite make it out.

Feeling almost numb with exhilaration, I settled back in the seat and looked around. We were whizzing by supermarkets and pool stores and a string of Circle Ks, heading straight for a mountain called Squaw Peak. The business district gave way to neighborhoods, then houses thinned out more and more the closer we got to the mountains, leaving only spindly cacti and greenish-gray scrub brush.

We turned onto a side road that wound around the mountain and through a small park at its base. Here and there people picnicked at shelters set up along the road, the smoke from their barbecues twisting into the sky. A few hikers lingered at the base of the main mountain path, sipping from water bottles.

"You're taking me climbing?" I asked, glancing at my watch. "Isn't it getting a little late for that?"

But Chris only smiled in response. At the crest of a hill, he U-turned and parked the car on the shoulder, facing down. From that height, we had a clear view of Phoenix, which is laid out like a grid. I traced Glendale Avenue westward past orchards and church steeples, and found where our apartment would be. Then, out of the corner of my eye, I sensed Chris staring at me. My pulse quickened as I flashed back to my daydream about his kissing me.

"Amy," Chris said, as he put his hand gently on my forearm. My skin got goose bumps even though I still had his sweatshirt on, but I kept my arm still. "Can I ask you a question?"

I nodded cautiously.

But before he could even finish saying, "What's going on with you and Rick Finnegan?" I was already blurting out, "Nothing. Really, nothing. He's a friend."

Chris looked relieved for a moment. Then his expression became serious again. "I know you guys are close, and if you're going out with him—"

"I'm not," I interrupted. "Going out with Rick, I mean. We've just been studying for the PSATs together."

I didn't think there was any way Chris could have heard that Rick had kissed me. It had just happened the night before, and my lukewarm response to Rick's kiss certainly wasn't something he would want to brag about to the guys.

"Then how about next Saturday?" Chris asked. He must have been nervous, because in one sentence his voice kept changing, like a radio being tuned, from high-pitched to deep and gravelly. "I know you're really busy, but how about going out with me?"

"Sure." I tried to sound cool about it, like I got asked out all the time. But inside, my heart was leaping.

I'd never even had a real date. Sure, I'd gone to the movies a few times with Rick, but that didn't count. He was more like a brother than a boyfriend.

Why hadn't I dated? I wasn't sure. I was smart and fairly interesting. In terms of looks I would have given myself a seven on a good hair day. Maybe an eight in the summer when I have a tan. I have thick blond hair that falls to my chin and almond-shaped blue eyes. Rick told me I was gorgeous a couple of weeks ago, but then again, his opinion isn't the one I'd trust.

Blythe said I probably seemed too busy with school and the Dolphins for a guy to bother asking me out. "You have to flash a red light," she was always saying, "to get a guy to brake." She said that I was stuck on yellow. I said I hadn't found anyone worth signaling to. Or the time to signal.

Until now.

I smiled at Chris, and he grinned as if he was really relieved I'd said yes. "Great!" he said.

I had to change the subject to keep from bouncing right out of my seat from excitement. "Okay, I give up," I told Chris, gesturing out into the desert around us. "What's this thing I have to see?"

"Any moment now," he said.

I thought about how much could change in a moment. A swimmer could slip from first place to second. A girl could fall in love, as my mom had, and ditch her plans for college. A boy like Rick could lose his mind and try to kiss you, when the last time you checked, you were just friends. Or you could discover your name written inside a boy's notebook, and never be able to look at him the same way again.

I was sure Chris would kiss me any second. But he didn't. He didn't put his arm around me, didn't move closer, or even close his eyes. Instead, he offered me a cheap pair of sunglasses he pulled out of the glove compartment. Then he donned his baseball cap, which he'd pulled out from under the front seat.

The sunglasses were too big, but I put them on and gave Chris a questioning look. "Here we go," Chris said, grinning at me.

The sun had continued to sink while we were driving, turning from yellow to red as it neared the horizon. It was so beautiful. The sun cast a red-orange stain across Chris's face, almost like an instant tan. He looked fantastic in that color, I thought, my heart thumping. Until that moment, I'd never noticed the freckles across the bridge of his nose or the brilliant gold flecks in his eyes.

Out there in the open, sitting next to him in a convertible at the base of Squaw Peak, I felt this incredible rush of happiness. Without realizing it, I gave a deep, contented sigh.

"Wow," I murmured.

"You got that right," said Chris, turning to me.

Then he turned back toward the sunset and stared, squinting, straight ahead.

I smiled. He thought I had meant the sunset.

"I've tried out lots of different views of the sun going down," Chris said. "But I think this one is definitely the best."

"Yes, it is," I agreed. "It's the most beautiful sunset I've ever seen."

I wasn't thinking about my homework, or even about the swim meet with the state champion Sharks. I wasn't thinking about the future at all. I was too busy taking in those few slow moments when the day turns to night.

Chapter Three

"FIVE CALLS!" I exclaimed, looking at the blinking answering machine in the front hallway of our apartment. Chris had just dropped me off, and I practically floated into the house.

The first message, the second, the third, and the fourth were all from Blythe, each one more frantic than the one before.

"Our health project! Oh, no," I said, hitting the side of my head with the palm of my hand. *That* was what I'd forgotten—to meet Blythe at the library! I looked at my watch and was surprised to see that it was seven o'clock, a full two hours after I had promised to meet her.

As the fifth message played, my mom walked into the house. "Hi, sweetie. The manager let me go early tonight," she said, stopping to listen. I was relieved that the last message wasn't from Blythe too. It was Rick.

"That Rick," Mom said. "Where has he been? I've missed seeing his face around here lately."

"Mmmm," I mumbled. *You only like him because you know he's just a friend*, I thought. My mom has lived in fear of the term *boyfriend* ever since I turned thirteen. I knew it was because in her senior year of high school she'd fallen in love with my father and gotten pregnant with me. They'd gotten married, and she had given up her plans for college. Then my father had gone, leaving her with no education, no job, and a little kid to raise on her own.

My mom always said that the women in our family have weak knees and crooked hearts, and that you can't let that get in the way of discipline and hard work. According to her, a girl has to be fast enough to dodge guys who'll take advantage of her, strong enough not to fall head-over-heels in love, and able to leap over her own mushy feelings in a single bound.

So you can see that I wasn't about to tell her that Chris and I watched the sunset together.

Mom's always thought of me as her treasure. I mean, when I was little she made all my baby clothes. It was cheaper for sure, but she claimed that nothing in the department stores was good enough for me. In grade school, she baked banana bread and cookies for my lunch box, when all I really wanted was the canned pudding and Oreos the other kids had.

Though we had trouble paying the rent sometimes, Mom still managed to scrape together money for an algebra tutor, racing suits for my competitions, and a summer membership to a private pool. And when I started high school, she took a second job to save for my college tuition. All my life, whenever I've thanked her, she's said, "You can thank me by getting the education I never did."

Needless to say, I didn't want her to know I'd blown off my health project either. Not exactly blown off, I told myself. Forgotten. I quickly pushed the erase button on the answering machine so she couldn't play back the messages from Blythe. I also didn't feel like telling her that the subject of our project was intimacy.

Mom turned toward the kitchen, then paused. "Are you interested in Rick?"

"Mom!" I said. "He's my friend! That's all."

"Just keep things in perspective," she warned me. "Remember, if brains and ambition were all it took to get a girl into college, by now your old mom would have her Ph.D."

"How could I forget it," I snapped, "when you keep reminding me?"

She looked as if she was going to say something else, but instead she turned and walked toward the kitchen. As soon as she was out of earshot, I picked up the phone to call my loyal (and, if she was mad enough, possibly my ex-best) friend Blythe.

"I was at the library all afternoon doing research for our project," Blythe fumed. "Where were you?"

"I'm sorry about the mix-up," I said apologetically. "I really meant to go there after practice, but I spaced it. Somehow my body just rebelled against my mind."

"Amy, did you get a personality transplant or something?" Blythe demanded, but to my relief, she laughed. "Since when do you go spacing things? Besides, couldn't your body at least have made it to a phone?"

"Blythe, don't be mad," I half whispered into the receiver, not wanting my mom to hear. "The truth is, I couldn't call you because I drove with Chris Shepherd up to Squaw Peak."

"Chris Shepherd?" Blythe couldn't contain her curiosity. "No way! Amy Wyse likes a guy? What's going on? Have you been holding out on me?"

Her questions were coming at me so quickly that I started laughing. I was dying to tell her about Chris, but I wasn't quite ready to tell her everything I was feeling. It was too new. So I said, "No, I haven't been holding out, and yes, I like him."

"Unbelievable," Blythe said. "How did it happen?"

"Well, weirdly enough, it kind of started when Rick kissed me after our final review session last night—"

"Wait a second," Blythe interrupted, sounding utterly perplexed. "How could you not tell me this? Rick kissed you? You kissed Rick?"

"Yeah, sort of, except it made me realize that I didn't want to kiss Rick at all. I mean, I couldn't. It did make me realize I kind of wanted to kiss somebody else, though."

Blythe let out her breath. "Amy, you really did have a personality transplant."

I laughed. "It sounds weird, doesn't it?"

"Completely," Blythe agreed. "But what about Rick? Why didn't you want to kiss him?"

"Because he's my pal—our pal. I can't really picture him in that way."

"Leave it to you to find fault with perfection," she said. "He's only the most together guy you know, not to mention the most talented writer and editor the *Thunder*'s ever had."

"No, you're the best writer," I said.

"But Rick's a serious writer," Blythe said.

"To me, that's his problem," I argued. "Rick's the kind of guy you tell your problems to, or eat chicken wings with, or bring home to your parents, not the kind you want to kiss."

Blythe wasn't buying it. She sighed. "I can't believe you. I can't believe this."

And that's when it hit me. "The way you're talking, Blythe," I said, "maybe you're the one who wants to hook up with Rick."

Blythe was silent for a moment, a telltale sign. "He's too busy going after you," she finally moaned. "He doesn't even know I'm alive."

"That's not true," I protested, but I had this funny feeling: half disappointment for my best friend, half stupid pride.

Blythe has long, straight, shiny blond hair and a great body. She's also smart and funny. She had gone out with one guy all last year, but they broke up over the summer, and she wasn't dating anyone now. I, on the other hand, who had never dated, suddenly had two guys wanting to go out with me.

"Anyway," Blythe said, changing the subject, "you're not getting off so easy. I put two books for our project on reserve for you: *Love and Mental Health* and *Psychological Theories of Intimacy*."

"Sounds pretty racy," I joked. "I'll have to cover them with plain brown paper so my mom won't see what I'm reading."

"Why don't you get the books tonight and come over here?" Blythe asked. "The library closes at nine."

"I don't want my mom to know I haven't started on the project yet," I whispered. "I'll pick them up tomorrow." Then I realized that we had a swim meet the next day. "Oh, I forgot. I have a meet tomorrow. But I'll pick them up the next day."

"Okay," Blythe agreed. "But I really want to get started on it soon. I know we have over a month, but there's a lot of work to do."

After I hung up the phone, I went to my room and unloaded my books onto my desk just like I always did. I kicked off my shoes and tossed them into my closet just like I always did. Just like always, I glanced over the careful list I'd made at the beginning of the week.

But when I opened up my physics book, the graphs and formulas somehow transformed into Chris's face—the way it looked in the warm, orangy light of the sunset. And when I finally put it aside and turned to my English notebook, I felt a delicious chill as my careful script turned into his loopy scrawling of my name over and over again.

So I got up from my desk and flopped on my bed, which I absolutely never did, and closed my eyes to relive every second of the afternoon I'd spent with Chris.

Chapter Four

I T WAS A well-known fact that Mr. Tayerle, our physics teacher, hated tardiness more than any other academic vice. He was a scientist, after all, and the stiff way he walked, talked, and graded our reports always gave me the feeling his whole life ticked along like a reliable wristwatch, digitally precise.

So I was worried the next day when, ten minutes into Tayerle's lecture on astronomy, Chris came into the room. He didn't enter quietly, smiling apologetically, as I would have done. Instead, he burst through the doorway and stood there a moment, glancing around as he tried to catch his breath.

"Uh-oh," Blythe whispered from the desk next to mine. She loved a good scandal, and she leaned back to watch the action unfold, a grin on her face.

"Uh-oh is right," I whispered back.

Chris appeared to be wearing the same torn Levi's and scuffed Doc Martens he had worn the day before. Only his navy T-shirt was different.

It had taken me forever that morning to get ready for school. I'd tried on a pair of black leggings, a lavender miniskirt, and then my faded denim overalls before I settled on my favorite jeans and a ribbed blue sweater. Somehow, every time I pictured my name in Chris's notebook, I headed right back to my closet. But Chris, apparently, hadn't suffered the same overnight attack of self-consciousness.

Blythe and I weren't the only ones staring. The whole class was watching quietly, wondering what Chris's excuse for being late was and what Mr. Tayerle would do. That's when Chris spotted the mobile of the universe the teacher had put out on display. He slapped a hand to his heart and pretended to fall back into the doorway, gripping the frame for support. "Someone stop the world from spinning," he said. "I want to get off."

"I'm afraid you're my captive for the next forty minutes," Tayerle said dryly, glancing from Chris to the wall clock. Then he added, "Funny you should mention spinning." There wasn't the slightest hint of amusement in his voice. "Today we're talking about the orbits of the planets, if you'll kindly take your seat."

"Cool," said Chris. As he passed by the mobile, he reached out and gave Saturn's rings a twirl.

Chris always asked interesting questions in class, and he wasn't at all afraid of disagreeing with teachers. As a result, he could get away with things that no one else could.

If Tayerle had been the sort of teacher who gave points for participation, Chris would have been the best student in the class. As it was, though, Rick Finnegan outranked him. That's because while Chris was sending Tayerle off on tangents, Rick was meticulously taking down every word he said. Rick was practically a professional note taker, with all the practice he'd had covering stories for the *Thunder*. The pages in his notebook were so crammed full that there probably wasn't room left for doodling anything—definitely not the name of a girl.

In fact, Rick was so diligent I wouldn't have been surprised if he'd written down what happened next: Chris sauntered down the aisle and dropped a note on my desk.

"Mr. Shepherd," Tayerle said, holding out his hand and beckoning, "don't think I didn't see that message you just delivered to Ms. Wyse. I'd like to believe it contains your ponderings about astronomy, but I've a feeling that this morning your mind is on other matters."

"But Mr. Tayerle," Chris argued, as he picked up the note from my desk and went to place it in the teacher's hand, "how can a guy know about the universe without first examining his heart?"

It was like one of those nightmares where you show up at school without your clothes on—everyone who'd been staring at Chris turned to stare at me. Meanwhile, to my horror, Mr. Tayerle fumbled with his bifocals, then unfolded the note.

"Ms. Wyse?" he asked when he'd finished reading. "Would you please do Mr. Shepherd the honor of joining him in—I hope I'm reading correctly—something called a carbo load?"

"Is that legal?" someone called out, and the whole class started to laugh.

"It—it just means carbohydrates," I stammered, my cheeks turning bright red. "It's a Dolphin tradition. We go out for a big lunch before every swim meet."

"Say yes, then," Tayerle said, sending a humbler Chris back to his seat. "And with your permission, Ms. Wyse, we'll continue our own tradition—that of talking about science, rather than romance, in class."

"Okay, yes," I said to the ceiling. I couldn't look at him.

Tayerle went back to his lecture, reading from his ancient notes. He looked up every now and then, as if to make sure that we were still awake.

Somehow, his droning voice had seemed tolerable until yesterday, when Chris had said that Tayerle didn't have any fire. Now I sat there trying to listen, but all I could think of was Chris.

I tried to steal a look at him by moving my eyes in his direction without moving my neck. He sat three rows ahead and one over, so my view of him was limited to parts: a sinewy arm, his strong jawline, that thick brown hair.

Then Tayerle lost his place, and the room was silent as twenty-five college-bound classmates used the momentary pause to catch up on their notes, taking down every single testable word. Chris and I were the only two who weren't frantically writing, whose heads weren't bent over our desks. Until yesterday, to tell you the truth, I would have been scribbling away with the rest of the class.

Chris turned around and caught me staring, as if he'd read my mind. My heart beat faster as he held up his notebook, so I could see the single word he'd written: *Sorry*. Meaning, I guessed, for the note. I blushed again, but I smiled and shrugged.

It was too bad that Tayerle was such a boring teacher, because the unit on astronomy we'd started that week was actually really interesting. Luckily, I'd read ahead a chapter in our textbook, so while he droned on about the planets, I stared at Chris out of the corner of my eye and entertained

41

myself with more interesting thoughts.

Until yesterday, my life, like the universe, had a certain order to it: school, swimming, homework, friends. Now I sensed this unfamiliar pull. It was exciting but a little scary too.

Tomorrow things will fall back into place, I told myself. Tomorrow I'd be note-taking with the best of them, rather than daydreaming about Chris. The feelings I'd been having these last two days were unfamiliar, maybe, but they weren't threatening. They didn't mean anything had to change.

Class dragged on for what seemed like hours. Then, just before the bell rang, Mr. Tayerle gave us an assignment to observe Saturday night's lunar eclipse.

"Since the eclipse will begin at twelve-oh-eight A.M.," he said, "the project requires two people— one person to record the moon phases and the other to make coffee to keep that person awake." I was surprised at Tayerle's attempt to be funny. "But seriously," he continued, as though we ever took him as anything but, "I'd like you to choose partners and write up your observations in the form of a lab report."

When Tayerle said the word "partner," Chris turned around in his desk and raised a questioning eyebrow at me. I swallowed hard. I pictured Chris and me together at midnight, staring up at the night

42

sky. Just the idea of it was incredibly romantic. I nodded.

A split second later, I remembered Blythe. Ever since junior high, we'd had an unwritten rule that anytime we were in the same class, we worked on school projects together. The last thing I wanted was to make her mad, especially after what had happened yesterday. But the absolute last, last, last thing I wanted was to give up the opportunity to watch the eclipse with Chris.

After class, I caught up with Blythe. "You should pair up with Rick," I advised her in a whisper. "It's the perfect time for you two to be alone."

Blythe was shaking her head. "My parents are dragging me up to our cabin in Payson this weekend," she said, sighing. "So I'll be gazing at the heavens alone. And unless you can come with us, I guess you'll just have to pair up with Chris."

There was hardly anything I liked more than driving with the Carlsons to Payson, wedged into the backseat with Blythe and her brother and grocery bags full of junk food. We sang stupid road songs, and sometimes we did crossword puzzles together or played word games. I loved being with a real family, one where there was a mother and a father and a brother. Mr. and Mrs. Carlson seemed to really love each other, and Blythe and her little brother Bill actually got along. The cabin itself was beautiful—tucked away in the mountains northwest of Phoenix, surrounded on three sides by a fragrant forest of pines. But to me, getting up there was at least half the fun.

Blythe knew as well as I did that my mom would let me go. She welcomed any opportunity to get me out of the city to breathe some fresh air. But just then, I would have given up a trip to Paris to spend Saturday night with Chris.

"I have to stay home this weekend and finish my English paper," I said. "Not to mention those two books for our report that I have to start reading."

Blythe looked hurt for a moment, but then she winked at me. "Okay, Amy," she said. "By Monday, I'm sure you'll be something of an expert on the subject of intimacy."

Chapter Five

As I'd explained to Mr. Tayerle, it was a tradition for some of the Dolphins to go for a premeet carbo load. That's when we piled into someone's car at lunch period and cruised Central Avenue's mile-long stretch of restaurants, a virtual buffet of fast food. Though I'd always liked our ritual of pizza and french fries and camaraderie, that day I'd secretly been hoping that Chris and I could carbo-load alone.

But when I got to my locker at lunchtime, there was Shannon O'Malley, one of the Dolphins. "So who's driving today?" she asked.

Before I could even answer, Chris came up behind me. "We're going in Zipperman's car," he said, meaning Mark Zimmerman. He had gotten the nickname Zipperman because he zipped along in the water, the fastest swimmer on our team after Chris. "John Horvath's driving too, but I think he already left. Zipperman's out in the parking lot, waiting for us in his Blazer."

"Sorry, Amy," Chris whispered, as if he'd been thinking the very same thing I had. "Zipperman caught me between classes and wouldn't let me say no."

"That's okay," I said, but I had to admit I felt disappointed. When Zipperman turned the car around and pulled up at the curb beside us, I was doubly disappointed to see who was sitting next to him in the front seat. It was Jill Renfrew, another junior who was always competing with me for the chance to swim the 100 free. I'd recognize her linebacker shoulders and hairless arms (she shaved them so she'd slide like a snake through the water) anywhere.

"Oh, no, it's Cutthroat," I said under my breath. That was the secret nickname Shannon had given her after she'd overheard her telling one of our teammates that she thought I should be benched for skipping practice one day last week. "What if this carbo load is just a ploy for Jill to slip poison into my food, so that I can't swim in the meet?" I asked Chris jokingly.

Chris had noticed that Jill and I didn't get along, but he didn't know she had stolen (or as she put it, "misplaced") my bathing cap before divisionals last season. And though I couldn't prove it, I suspected she'd once cut the straps on my suit. He wrapped his arm around me conspiratorially as Shannon opened the car door and climbed into the backseat. "Don't eat anything she's touched," he whispered. "And if it'll make you feel safer, I'll taste your food before you eat."

I laughed like we were just buddies, but as I climbed into the car beside Shannon, I could feel goose bumps rising where his arm had been.

"Wait up!" someone called out. It was a hoarse, asthmatic voice I recognized as Wayne Dean's. Poor Wayne carried his inhaler everywhere. He seemed to be wheezing constantly, but amazingly, he breathed freely for the few minutes when he was swimming in a meet.

"Haul it, Dean," Zipperman said. "We've got a lot of food to consume in fifty minutes."

When we moved over to make room for him, my right leg was pushed against Chris's, and there was only a half inch of air between his shoulder and my face. A few weeks ago I might not have noticed, but now I was almost overwhelmed by his closeness. The electricity between us seemed miraculous to me.

Did this happen all the time between people? Is this what I had been missing? While I had been charging through swim meets and classes, racking up the trophies and the A's, other people had been falling in love? It was a completely new idea to me. It was like putting on a pair of glasses and suddenly seeing the world in a whole new set of colors.

"Everyone set?" Zipperman called out, enjoying his role as the pilot of this mission. In unison, we replied with our carbo-load cry, "Let's eat to beat!"

"All right," he said. "First stop: Pie in the Sky Pizzeria."

While we drove, Zipperman and Jill fought over the radio, trying to find a decent station. Shannon and Wayne were digging in their pockets, pooling their money for a first course of pizza. I was barely aware of all this commotion going on around me, I was so focused on that half inch between Chris and me.

"So—what do you want to do Saturday?" Chris asked, his breath tickling my ear.

I was confused by his question. "The assignment is to—"

"I don't mean the eclipse," he said. "I mean before that, for our date."

If he was asking for a list of romantic possibilities, I wasn't exactly the authority. "A movie?" I suggested weakly to the seat in front of me. I found it impossible to look at him directly. My face was so close to his that I might have kissed him accidentally if I'd turned forty-five degrees.

I stopped breathing as he studied the side of my face. "I'd rather look at you," he said so softly I wasn't sure I'd heard him.

I blushed and punched him lightly on his kneecap, a real sixth-grade thing to do. "Ouch!" he said, catching my hand in his and laying it flat across his heart. "Feel that—I'm wounded." He laughed, and I felt the tension of the moment subside.

"Take her to the greyhound races," Wayne Dean suggested.

"Don't listen to him," Shannon said. "That's the last place you want to go."

I hadn't even known they were listening, but now everyone started tossing out ideas.

"Dinner at the Coyote," Shannon continued. "Enchiladas by candlelight."

"Rollerblading," Jill suggested.

Oh, right, I thought. She'd love it if I broke my legs.

"Tubing on the Verde River," Zipperman tried.

None of their ideas struck me as quite right. I imagined something different—somewhere romantic but off the beaten path, a place where we could talk. Then Chris squeezed my hand. "How about a picnic on the rooftop of your apartment?" he whispered. "It's quiet, secluded, and a perfect place to watch the eclipse."

49

"Perfect," I agreed softly, wanting to keep our plans a secret from our teammates. Fortunately, at that moment we pulled up to the curb of Pie in the Sky, and the group was distracted by the prospect of pizza.

"Pay up," said Zipperman, passing around a rubber Dolphins swimming cap to take up a collection. "A large vegetarian costs nine bucks. That's a buck-fifty each."

Everyone dug into their wallets. One by one, we tossed dollar bills and bounced quarters into the cap.

"The smallest I've got is a twenty," Jill said when the cap was passed to her. "Can someone chip in for me, and I'll pay you back?"

Jill said the same thing every time we carboloaded, and all of us had taken turns paying her way. I would have thought she didn't have any money if she didn't wear a new outfit practically every day and if I hadn't seen her trying to use her parents' credit card to buy a soda and a sandwich at the school snack bar. I guess when you're as rich as some of the kids at Thunderbird, you just can't be bothered carrying petty cash.

"You can have my slice," I said. "I think I'll pass."

"Is your stomach bothering you, Amy?" Jill asked in a tone of false concern.

"No, ma'am," I said, winking at Chris. "Just

holding out for a burrito supreme."

Jill thought about that a moment. "What a coincidence—I suddenly got a craving for the exact same thing," she said.

"She must think that's your secret power food," Chris whispered.

"Fine by me," Zipperman said. "I say we get a medium instead of a large, and add one extra topping."

"Sausage," said Shannon.

"I'm allergic," Wayne wheezed.

"Zipperman, you have a microscopic memory," Chris said. "We started getting vegetarian because no one can agree on meats."

"I say we give the driver veto power," Zipperman suggested. "How about pepperoni?"

"In that case," I said, taking another dollar out of my wallet, "I will take a slice. Pepperoni works like a good-luck charm for me."

"Good-luck charm?" Jill asked.

I could see she was aching to go in on the pizza, but Zipperman was already on his way into the restaurant. She rolled down her window as if to call to him, then rolled it back up. She took out her wallet and put it back into her shoulder bag again. When Zipperman came back with the pizza, she whipped out the crumpled twenty and held it out to him so that it flapped in the air-conditioning breeze. "Is it too late to change my mind?" she asked. "I could just pay for the whole pizza—I probably owe everyone here at least a buck."

"Six," Shannon said.

"About three," said Zipperman.

"Two," Chris and I said in unison.

"Four-fifty, if you're going to bring it up," Wayne added.

"Okay, okay, I get the message!" Jill exclaimed, handing over the money to Zipperman. "Here's for the pizza, and keep the change. This carbo load's on me."

By our fourth stop, Taco Villa, the car was filled with greasy wrappers and the smell of pizza and french fries. We'd already stuffed ourselves to the gills when Zipperman declared that nachos-to-go were the one last thing the Dolphins needed to help us win the meet. I no longer wanted a burrito supreme.

At Taco Villa, the drive-through line was bumper-to-bumper with kids from our high school, some probably as hungry as we'd been two meals ago.

"There's no way we're waiting in that line," Zipperman said. He started to turn the car around.

"But the restaurant's almost empty," Chris pointed out. "If you park, we could go in and whip through the order line in three minutes, max."

"I'll go," I volunteered. I felt like I needed some fresh air.

"I'll go with you," Chris said.

The restaurant was cool and quiet, compared with the smoking asphalt of the parking lot and the noise of engines roaring outside. For a moment, we stood swaying slightly in the doorway, stunned by the blast of chilly air-conditioning.

"What a relief," I said, meaning that we were inside in the cool air, but also that we were, for a few minutes at least, alone.

"Yeah, it is," Chris said. The way he smiled at me I knew he was thinking the same thing I was.

We stepped up to the counter, and I ordered the nachos.

"I could wolf down a couple of tacos," Chris said, eyeing the menu.

"I hope you're kidding," I said. "You'd sink as soon as you hit the water!"

"At least I'd drown happy," he joked. "But seriously, lately I've had this monster appetite."

"Is that why you were late to physics this morning?" I couldn't resist asking. "You were polishing off a six-course breakfast?"

Chris laughed. "Actually," he said, "I was having this great dream I didn't want to wake up from. I must have shut off my alarm clock and gone back to sleep."

"I've done that," I told him. "Last week, I was

dreaming I got these fat acceptance letters from twenty different universities. It was the best feeling—then my mom came in the room and turned on the light, yelling, 'Rise and shine!' and it hit me that I haven't even decided where I want to apply yet." I stopped for a moment. "What did you dream?"

"W-well, uh," he stammered, "we were driving in the Mustang with the top down . . ."

I felt my cheeks flush. "We?" I asked.

"Um, yeah," he said. "You and I."

You and I. Those words seemed to hang in the air between us. I looked at the menu above the counter, then at the floor, then out the window. When I finally got up the courage to look at Chris's face, he was smiling ruefully.

"Great," he said with a forced laugh. "I'm dreaming about you, and you're dreaming about college. What's wrong with this picture?"

I gave a feeble laugh as I gazed at the floor. Was there something wrong with this picture?

Chris wasn't very talkative during the hour-long bus ride to Ocotillo High, the home of the Sharks. We sat across the aisle from each other, pretending to be absorbed in our homework. Still, whenever I raised my head to keep from getting carsick, I saw that Chris was looking at me.

I was so busy trying not to look up too often

that I got absolutely no work done.

By the time we got to Ocotillo, the pool was such a welcome sight that I didn't even have my usual premeet nerves. I couldn't wait to change into my racing suit and step up to the starting block.

"Good luck, Amy," Chris said, putting his hand on my arm, before he headed for the boys' locker room. "I'll be rooting for you."

"Thanks," I said, a flutter of nervousness in my chest. "I'll do the same for you."

In the girls' locker room, I changed into my suit and stuffed my sweats and tennis shoes into my team bag. Then, instead of going out to the pool with the other girls, I decided to stay in the locker room and practice imagining my flip turn until the meet began. I sat down on a bench and closed my eyes.

"Are you saying a prayer?" a voice interrupted, and I looked up to see Jill Renfrew pacing around in a pair of ankle weights she always wore up until the very moment she jumped into the pool.

"Sort of," I said.

She frowned. "Maybe I should do that too."

It was hard to hate somebody who was so insecure she didn't trust herself to be herself, but tried instead to be just like you. I sort of felt sorry for her.

55

That feeling disappeared, however, when we took our places on the starting block for the 100-meter freestyle and she scowled at me. "Just make sure you stay out of my lane," she ordered. I rolled my eyes. There were three good swimmers from Ocotillo swimming this event, and I had to worry about being demoralized by my own teammate.

"Don't worry. I don't flail as much as you do," I said. "I prefer to swim in a straight line."

Standing on the block in those few tense moments before the whistle, I scanned the crowded, noisy room for Chris. When I caught his eye, he smiled. I suddenly felt weirdly self-conscious. Did I look funny in my racing suit? Was I so completely unsexy in my cap and goggles that he'd wish he'd never asked me out?

"On your marks," announced the timer, and I bent my knees and leaned forward, toes curled on the block's edge. In the moment before the buzzer sounded, the gym grew so quiet I could hear the tick of the time clock and my own steady breathing. I looked toward the wall at the end of the lane and tried to picture a perfect flip turn, but I felt the nervous trembling in my legs.

"You can do it, Amy!" I heard Chris shout, or maybe I just thought I did.

Then the buzzer sounded and I was airborne, stretching my body from my fingers to my toes.

For a moment, I forgot about everything—the other swimmers, Mom's expectations, the huge health project . . . Chris. I was suspended, waiting for the thrilling moment when I'd hit the pool's surface.

I entered the water smoothly and was off. I could hear the familiar *swish, swish, swish* of the water in my ears. Swimming is so automatic that your mind is free to wander as you skim along pulled by a zing of adrenaline, air bubbles escaping and tickling your face. *Go, go, go,* I told myself, feeling this pulsating beat in my body.

Turn, I said to myself on the first lap, and I pushed off beautifully. *Turn,* I said on the second, and my body obliged gracefully. On the third lap I felt joyous, and let myself imagine for a second Coach August posting my name on the board above our home pool, the one that boasted the school's best times. All I had to do, I was thinking as I approached the end of the pool, was remember not to . . .

Whack!

I began the last lap awkwardly, my heels stinging and my confidence bruised from my too-familiar encounter with the lip of the pool.

But when I raised my head I was in first. I'd won! It was just like my daydreams, even after the disastrous third lap. I left Jill and the three Ocotillo swimmers blinking in the water as I hoisted myself out.

I saw Chris smiling at me and I smiled back. I felt great.

"Congratulations again," Chris said, settling into the seat next to me on the bus to take us back home after the meet. He seemed happy with his three second places, even though he didn't swim his best times. "You swam an incredible hundred."

"Thank you" was the only thing I could think of to say.

"Your flip turn is getting better."

I shrugged. "Two out of three, anyway."

He reached over and pushed my wet hair from my face. The gentle touch of his fingers lingered on my skin. "You're tough, Amy." He studied my face for another second and smiled. "Beautiful, too."

It was a perfect moment, sitting there in the darkness of the bus, the yellow glow of a streetlamp lighting Chris's face.

"After wearing my ankle weights, I felt like I was flying," Jill's voice droned from the seat in front of us, breaking the fragile moment. "It was my best time ever," she bragged.

I smiled at Chris. Maybe it was because I was feeling so buoyant, but I was genuinely happy for Jill.

I was genuinely happy period. I had won my most important race. I was well on my way to the scholarship I had been dreaming about for three years. My leg was pressed against the leg of the most wonderful guy I had ever met, a guy who thought I was beautiful.

I felt right then like I could have everything in the world.

Chapter Six

"COME BY OUR apartment at eleven," I told Chris on Friday, scribbling the address on a piece of notebook paper. Even though he had dropped me off there, I figured he might not remember the exact address. I definitely didn't want him to get lost. "We're in apartment number five. My mom will be sleeping, so don't ring the doorbell. I'll wait for you outside."

I decided right then not to even risk asking my mom if I could go on our "date." I had a feeling she wouldn't understand that this was an assignment, especially since it started at midnight. Anyway, on Saturdays she worked until nine in the evening, and she went to bed soon after she got home from work.

But not that Saturday. When she got home from

working at the supermarket, Mom was peppier than usual. She'd recently had her annual review at the bank, and today she'd learned that the manager had given her a raise. "We're not millionaires yet," she said as she unloaded groceries she'd picked up during her El Rancho break. "But every bit gets you one step closer to college."

"Oh, Mom, congratulations! That's wonderful," I told her, giving her a hug. As I watched her dance around the kitchen, her partner a package of flour, I felt a sharp pang of guilt. After all she'd done for me, I was planning a secret rendezvous with a guy she'd never met.

"Don't you look pretty," she said to me, when she'd dropped the flour on the table and come over to where I was sitting. "And you smell nice, too. What's the occasion?"

I glanced up quickly, plucking at the green linen shirt I'd worn in honor of my date. "No occasion." It came out as kind of a squeak. "I mean, just your raise," I added lamely.

She stared at me with one eyebrow raised for about ten seconds before she dug into her grocery bags.

"You must be exhausted," I said, getting up to help her.

"Not at all," she replied, producing a plastic bag full of apples. "In fact, I thought we'd celebrate our good fortune by making a big apple pie."

"Pie?" I looked at my watch—it was already nine fifteen. "You'll be asleep before it's out of the oven," I said doubtfully, watching her dart around the kitchen, pulling out ingredients, a rolling pin, and a pie tin. She was acting as if it were first thing in the morning and she had a full tank of energy.

Mom put her hands on her hips and gave me a mock frown. "What's gotten into you, Amy? You sound like my mother, telling me it's past my bedtime."

"It is," I said, yawning as I turned on the oven and got out the butter to grease the pie tin. If she was determined to bake at this unlikely hour, there was no stopping her. The least I could do was to speed the project along. "I'll do the filling," I said, "if you'll make the crust."

As I worked, I mentally counted up the minutes: a half hour to make the filling if I peeled and cored and cut the apples fast. Add an hour more to bake, which would bring us up to ten forty-five. Even if we saved the pie for tomorrow, quarter to eleven was cutting it close. If I turned up the oven temperature a notch or two, would the pie bake faster or would it just burn?

"Besides," Mom said as if continuing a conversation she'd started in her head, "we'll need a snack if we want to stay up for the lunar eclipse."

I nearly choked on the piece of apple I was

munching. Right before she said it, I'd been debating whether or not to tell her about the physics assignment. But just then, the prospect of telling her went from risky to too late.

"Oh," I said dumbly. "I didn't know you were planning to watch the eclipse."

"Come on, Amy, can't you show a tad more enthusiasm?" Mom complained as she plunged her hands into the mixing bowl, working the lard into the flour. "It only happens once every few years."

"I am excited," I protested glumly. "It's just that . . . it's so late." Meanwhile, my mind was racing. What would I do when Mom and I were outside at midnight looking moonward and Chris just happened to show up? I couldn't very well call him, and risk waking up his parents, to tell him the whole thing was off. Desperately, I thought of suggesting that Mom and I watch from the apartment pool out back, so we wouldn't run into Chris, who'd be waiting out front. I was thinking I could hang a banner from my bedroom window that said, "Chris—I have to cancel. Something urgent came up."

While I was scheming like a criminal, trying not to act nervous but throwing glances at the oven clock, Mom was humming and pinching her piecrust into a delicate scalloped edge. She was never as happy as when she was baking, which she

64

rarely got to do. That and classical music were the two things that helped her relax.

"How about some classical music while we wait?" I suggested while she put the pie in the oven. I went to the kitchen counter and turned on the radio.

"Since when are you willing to switch from the rock-and-roll station?" She laughed. "No, thanks, it'll make me too sleepy. Let's clean up the mess we've made, then find something lively on TV instead."

By that point, I was the one who was exhausted, mostly from being so nervous. When we finished cleaning up, I dragged my feet to the living room and flipped through the TV channels, looking for something that would put Mom to sleep. An old movie maybe, one she'd seen at least a dozen times. I'd have settled for a rerun of a sitcom—anything, really, as long as it wouldn't keep Mom on the edge of her seat.

"Listen, the late movie sounds terrific," Mom said, pressing a finger to a column in *TV Guide*. "'Based on a true story: Mother launches a nation-wide search for her daughter, who disappeared under suspicious circumstances.'"

For a minute, I thought she was teasing, that somehow she'd found out about my plans to "disappear" with Chris. But when I turned to the channel she told me to, I saw it was a real show, "Bring My Daughter Back."

We settled down on the sofa, while in the kitchen the oven timer tick-ticked away. "Let's turn the lights off, so it's like a real movie," I said, reaching for the lamp.

"Okay," she said with a yawn.

Despite the action-packed plot of the movie, thirty minutes into it and two minutes before the pie was done, Mom had curled up on the couch and fallen fast asleep. Moving carefully so as not to wake her, I stood and turned off the TV. In the semidarkness, I pulled a blanket from the linen closet and tucked her in from neck to feet. Then I tiptoed into the kitchen and quietly turned off the oven timer.

When I took the steaming, bubbling pie out of the oven, my mouth watered from the spicy-sweet smell that filled the kitchen. And even though I'd been looking forward to meeting Chris, I felt a twinge of regret that tonight wouldn't be as simple as Mom and I sharing a piece of hot, homemade apple pie. I had this funny feeling that nothing after that night ever would.

Chapter Seven

OUTSIDE IT WAS breezy and warm, shorts-and-T-shirt weather, the kind of night that feels more like the end of summer than the middle of fall. But as Mom says, that's Arizona for you, with its two seasons: hot and even hotter. Sometimes I wished I lived in a more changeable climate, a place that had the brilliant-colored leaves and snowscapes we'd been taught to draw in second grade. But that night I was happy being just where I was. I felt content sitting in the square of grass outside our apartment, breathing in the scent of eucalyptus and cooling earth, watching the wind fan the branches of the spindly palm trees above me. Waiting for Chris.

He showed up at exactly eleven, turning the corner of our street pedaling a bike. Around the handlebars, he'd strapped a blanket and a wicker picnic basket. "My mom packed this for us. Cokes and brownies," he said, jumping lightly off his seat. He unleashed the basket from the bike and handed it to me. "You know, to help us stay awake."

I felt envious for a boy's life then, in which you could walk out the front door at eleven with your mother's goodie basket and blessing, instead of stuffing your bed with clothes to look like a sleeping body (as I had) and tiptoeing out. I was afraid Chris would think I was a baby if he knew I hadn't gotten permission, so I didn't tell him.

"How come you didn't drive?" I asked instead. In fact, I was curious why a guy whose family had money didn't have his own car.

"You promise you won't think I'm a dork?" he asked.

I couldn't imagine what he was going to say. "I promise."

"I just think that the less we pollute the environment, the better." Then he added quickly, "I'm not a fanatic or anything. I love driving my brother's car, and if I get into Stanford next year, I'll get a car. But if I don't need a car, why buy one?" He shrugged.

"I think that's great," I said sincerely.

He seemed embarrassed, and he looked up at

our apartment. "You have a nice place."

"Thanks," I said, but I could tell that he was trying to be nice. The Palms apartments aren't exactly luxurious. They're a series of slightly rundown two-story buildings with balconies, forty years old, as old as just about anything in Phoenix ever got before some new developer came in and tore it down. Chris's family, on the other hand, lived in a neighborhood full of new houses, huge Tudor and French château mansions. I knew that because the swimming bus had dropped him off there after a few late meets.

I led him around to the tiny side yard. We stashed his bike in the oleanders, dragged an old ladder from its resting place in the crabgrass, and leaned it up against the side of the house. "Be careful of the roof tiles," I whispered as I began carefully climbing. "There were a few loose the last time I was up."

"You've been up here before?" Chris asked, following my slow steps up the ladder, the blanket around his shoulder and the picnic basket tucked under his arm. "And here I thought I was being so original."

"Well, I've never been up here *with* anyone before," I said. "It's a good place to think. You can see a lot of the neighborhood—though not the whole city, the way you can from Squaw Peak."

We climbed onto the gently sloping rooftop,

spread out the blanket, and settled down to watch the sky. I couldn't help feeling grateful that my mom was asleep on the first floor, rather than right below us. Chris lay back against the roof. I sat up straight beside him, my arms wrapped around my knees.

Chris looked adorable in his baggy shorts and baseball T-shirt. I felt strangely calm sitting next to him. My heart wasn't hammering, like it was the day we watched the sunset together, and my palms were dry. I'd never done anything like this in my life, but somehow it felt perfectly right.

"Fifty-three minutes to show time," I said, squinting at my glow-in-the-dark wristwatch. Tayerle had told us that at 12:08 A.M., the moon would slowly move into the Earth's shadow. Since this was an entire lunar eclipse, the full moon would be totally in shadow. I knew from our astronomy book that the eclipse could last over three hours.

"Let's synchronize our watches," Chris said.

"Eleven fifteen," I said, and Chris answered, "Check."

We were quiet for a few minutes looking up at the sky. "This sort of reminds me of camping," Chris said finally. "The darkness, the quiet, the whole sky spread out above you . . ."

"The backache you have in the morning from sleeping on the ground . . ."

Chris laughed, and readjusted his body on the hard, jutting tiles. "All we need to make it perfect is some poison ivy and a few mosquitoes. I remember once, when I was a Boy Scout—"

"*You* were a Boy Scout?" I interrupted.

Chris propped himself up on one elbow. "Went all the way to Eagle," he said.

"No way!"

"Why don't you believe me?"

"I just can't see you in one of those little uniforms," I said. "I mean, don't you lose merit points or something if you have holes in your pants?"

Chris sat up then and tried to look indignant but then let a grin escape. "I'll tell you, wearing that uniform was beat. But my parents were always too busy being lawyers to take my brother and me camping. If it hadn't been for Boy Scouts, I might never have gotten out of Phoenix or learned the names of the stars."

"I didn't know both your parents were lawyers," I said.

"Yeah," Chris said, but he didn't sound too impressed. "And they're waiting for one of their children to follow in their footsteps. My brother Dave wants to join the Peace Corps, so I guess they're thinking I'm their man." He hesitated. "But I know I'm not."

"Mmm," I said, thinking of how I sometimes

71

felt I was living my mother's derailed dreams. "What do you want to do?"

Chris opened the wicker basket and pulled out two Cokes. "Well, I had this incredibly cool job last summer. I worked for the Habitat for Humanity building houses for low-income families," he said thoughtfully. "I'm signed up to do it again this summer, but considering I don't get paid anything, I guess it's not a practical choice for a career." He shrugged and handed me a Coke. "If we stay up here talking long enough, maybe you'll help me figure it out."

"I'll try," I said, reaching into the basket. "But first I'll need a little help from these brownies."

Chris's mom had stacked the brownies four across and three deep, and wrapped them first in plastic, then in aluminum foil. Chris tore the package open, making no effort to be neat about it. I thanked him for the brownie he offered, then took a big bite.

"This is delicious," I said. "Tell your mom she's a terrific baker."

"Oh, my mom didn't bake these," he said. "She's too busy to bake. She bought them at Sutton's."

I was silent, thinking of my mom baking an apple pie after working two jobs. "Well, they're still really good," I said.

"Mmm," Chris said, his mouth full of brownie.

"So what do you think about when you're sitting up here?" he asked.

"Oh, a bunch of things," I answered, trying to talk without chewing. "What college will be like, all the books I haven't read . . . lots of things. Sometimes I even count up all the trash cans in the neighborhood and try to imagine where all of it goes."

I didn't tell him that I also thought about what love means and whether marriage can last, and why my father had abandoned us so long ago. You couldn't tell a guy something that personal on your first date.

"Garbage! Now there's something that'll blow your mind," Chris said. "At our house we recycle everything, but it doesn't make a dent in what's thrown away. I really worry about what's happening to our environment and how we can solve the problems we're creating with all our waste."

"I do too," I said. "But somehow, up here, all problems seem solvable. Maybe it's because I'm looking down on them."

"Yeah," Chris said. "I know exactly what you mean."

Blythe and I were always finishing each other's sentences or punctuating them with "Exactly!," but I had never expected that to happen with a guy.

73

We sat talking, eating, and watching the moon until finally we noticed that one side of it was changing shape. Twenty minutes later it was totally in eclipse.

Even though I had read all about eclipses, I was still surprised that the moon hadn't disappeared in blackness. Instead, it was a dull coppery color. It was eerie but also comforting, like the gentle glow of a child's night-light. "Amazing!" I said. "I expected it to look much darker."

"It is amazing," Chris said. "Some of the sunlight that shines on Earth is scattered by our atmosphere, and enough of that light reaches the moon." He laughed. "I don't think Tayerle would be too pleased with my nontechnical explanation."

"Who cares?" I said softly. "It's magical."

"Well, enjoy the magic," Chris said. "The moon will only be in total eclipse for seven minutes."

I stood up then like a surfer, half crouched, legs bent at the knees.

"Where are you going?" Chris asked.

"I just want to check something." I waddled like that to the roof's peak, and after securing my footing, made my way cautiously down the slight slope on the other side. The back end of our apartment overlooked the courtyard all the Palms tenants shared: a half circle of Bermuda grass and a medium-sized lima-bean-shaped pool.

74

"Chris, come over here," I whispered. When I called him, he stood quickly, waving his arms in the air for balance. "Careful," I warned him, hunkering down again into the surfer position. "You have to walk like this."

Chris joined me at the roof's edge, and I pointed to the pool. There, reflected in the surface of the still water, was the coppery orb of the moon.

"Wow," we both said.

It was one of those perfect moments that you tuck away to look at later, like rose petals pressed between the pages of a book. I remember the joy in Chris's expression and the warm breeze that carried the scent of pool chlorine. The moon looked so real floating there in the water that it seemed you could dive in and retrieve it with your bare hands.

Then Chris put his arm around me and pulled me close to him. "Amy," he whispered, "I've liked you for such a long time, ever since you first joined the—" But before he could finish his sentence, I linked my fingers around his neck and stopped him with a kiss.

His lips were firm, like in my daydream, and chocolate-brownie sweet. I could feel them humming against mine, as if they held some secret. Before, I'd always worried about the technicalities of kissing, like how to avoid bumping noses.

Now I found that everything, even noses, fit together, without my even trying. Chris opened his mouth slightly, tasting my lips with tiny, gentle bites.

Around us, the night was alive with the late-night sound that my neighborhood makes, the pulse and hum of a hundred pool pumps. This solemn sound and the kiss made me restless, the way quiet hymns played in church sometimes make me want to shout. Or maybe I should blame the full moon for what happened next.

I broke away from Chris and blurted out—I can't explain why—"I dare you to jump in the pool!"

Chris peeled his T-shirt off before I could say I was joking. He tossed it down into the courtyard and stood there peering over the roof's edge, silently calculating the distance from there to the pool.

"Wait—are you sure you can make it?" I whispered.

"If I don't," he said theatrically, "at least the last thing I see will be you." With that, he swung his arms out and leapt from the roof. Midair, he hugged his legs to his chest and cannonballed safely into the pool.

When he hit, the moon's reflection exploded into pieces, then rippled back together. Water crashed on the deck, and the lounge chairs that surrounded it. I waited with my breath held, until finally Chris's head popped up to the surface. "Come on in!" he stage-whispered, dog-paddling in place. "The water feels great!"

I imagined my mother's voice warning me not to take chances even as I tossed my sneakers over and stood there, shivering, in my bare feet. Then I heard Blythe say that I was too cautious, that I'd never get anywhere if I lived my life stuck at a yellow light. I closed my eyes for a second and took a deep breath. "Now or never," I said out loud.

Then I opened my eyes and dove into the darkness, aiming for the reflection of the moon. But instead of pulling a noisy cannonball, as Chris had, I sliced straight into the water and hardly made a splash.

"The water doesn't feel great!" I complained. "It's cold." It was hard to keep quiet with my teeth chattering so hard.

Chris kept treading water and swimming in circles like a dog. "It helps if you keep moving," he said.

Relieved that I had made it into the pool, I swam to the edge quickly and hoisted myself out onto the deck. "Let's get out of here before the manager sees us," I whispered. *Or my mom hears us,* I added silently. "Follow me—there are plenty of other pools we can hop."

★　　★　　★

If you've never heard of pool hopping, you should come to Phoenix, where it's practically a varsity sport. If you grew up here, you've done it: climbed over backyard fences, tiptoed across evergreen Bermuda-grass lawns, and tried out other people's pools. I, for one, could tell you the size and shape and water temperature of every pool on our block. But I hadn't hopped a pool since eighth grade, hadn't even thought of it until the moon made me crazy, until some wild, reckless urge got into me that night.

"Come on," I whispered to Chris as we made our way, dripping and shivering, into our front yard. Chris hopped on one foot behind me, grabbing his other, soggy-sneakered foot with both hands. I noticed then that he'd jumped into the Palms pool without taking his shoes off. "Hold on a minute," he said, pouring water out of a heel and onto the lawn.

"Let's do Joey Favata's," I said, pointing to a ranch-style house at the far end of our street.

"Should be good," Chris said, slinging his sneakers over his shoulder and holding on to them by their laces. "His dad's a real hothead." Chris knew as well as I did that only part of the point of hopping pools was getting wet. Most of the fun came from almost getting caught.

We started off down the street toward the

Favatas', moving slowly and cautiously at first, then sprinting boldly from lamppost to lamppost. Like burglars, we avoided the greenish light of the streetlamps, trying to keep to the safety of the darkness in between. There were lights on in a few houses—probably people who'd watched the eclipse—but at that hour of the morning, most of the neighborhood was already asleep.

At the Favatas', the windows were dark, but four floodlights shone across the yard in green and blue and red. We darted through the circus colors and slipped around back to the six-foot stucco wall.

"Here's a foothold," I whispered, pulling back a tangle of crabgrass to reveal a palm tree stump. Chris put his bare foot there and reached for the top of the wall. "Any dogs?" he turned to ask me before he lifted himself up.

Yapping dogs were a challenge to pool hoppers—right up there with creaky gates and the crunching sound of someone walking across a desert lawn. "No dogs," I reassured him. "And it's grass on the other side, so you won't cut your feet when you land."

"Good to know," Chris said. He boosted himself up to the top of the fence and sat there a moment, surveying the yard. "It's a great pool," he said admiringly. "They've got a water slide and a Jacuzzi and a plastic shark raft."

"Move over," I said. "Let me get up."

Just as I pulled myself up to sit beside him, a light went on in one of the windows, the one that I guessed was the bathroom. The sound of running water followed, and Chris and I waited nervously until the light went off again. "Hold on a sec," Chris said, grabbing my arm as I made a move to jump into the yard. "We don't know for sure yet that the person's back in bed."

"Where's your sense of adventure?" I teased him.

Chris looked at me like I was nuts. "I must have left it back on your roof."

Actually, I was bluffing. The reason I was in a hurry to get going was that I knew any Favata who happened to glance out a window had a perfect view of us balanced there on the wall. I didn't want to alarm Chris, but the longer we sat there waiting, the more we were sitting ducks.

"Besides," I said, my teeth starting to chatter, "I've got to keep moving, to keep from freezing in my tracks."

Chris watched the window for a moment, tapping his heel on the stucco and biting his lower lip. Then he seemed to shrug off his worry. "I'll race you to that shark," he said.

With that, the two of us dropped, like overripe fruit, onto the soft grass. Chris took off in front of me, pausing only to spin a few cartwheels before he

80

reached the pool. Watching him leap and flail across the lawn made me laugh, but I really lost it when he dove toward the plastic shark open-armed. I watched in disbelief as he landed on his belly on the pool toy, and began to wrestle with the sea creature's giant dorsal fin.

By then, I was laughing so hard I could hardly walk. I managed to get to the pool's edge and practically fell in, right beside the shark.

Just as quickly, we were out again, whooping as we skipped across the brick patio, both hoping and fearing that someone would hear. We cackled like ghouls as we crossed the lawn and hurried to boost ourselves back over the wall.

I got to the wall before Chris did. "Oh, no!" I said when I suddenly realized there was no foothold.

"Put your foot here," Chris urged me, offering a step stool he'd made by joining his hands.

"But who will help you?" I asked him as I pulled myself up. I swung one leg over to straddle the wall and anxiously looked down at him.

"You will," he said. He pushed a foot against the wall for leverage and then reached up to grab my hands. "Come on, you can do it," he told me. "You're the strongest girl I know."

I could feel my calves scraping stucco as I gripped the wall tighter, one leg tensely anchored on each side. I tried not to panic, but I could see light after light going on inside the Favatas' house.

"One, two, three, *pull*," we said together.

My arms strained in their sockets, and for one scary moment, I felt myself tip toward the wrong side of the wall. I almost let go out of fear when I heard a door open. A second later, a man's angry voice called out, "Hey!"

"What was that?" Chris said, as if we didn't both know. I looked, and there was Mr. Favata in a plaid bathrobe, standing on the patio.

"It's Mr. Favata—he's coming over!" I shrieked. Chris's feet scrambled frantically, like an insect's, against the wall.

Just then adrenaline shot through me, like the zing I feel sometimes in the last lap of a race. All of a sudden, I couldn't feel how much my arms ached and how my legs stung. I pulled, and I practically launched Chris right over that wall.

We tumbled down together, laughing, out of breath, still holding hands.

"You're awesome," Chris said.

"No problem," I panted. "Now let's get out of here."

Back at the Palms we collapsed in the court-yard, still laughing and wheezing from running so hard. Then Chris climbed up to the roof and re-trieved the blanket and the wicker basket. Once he was on the ground, he wrapped the blanket around us both. "Do you think he recognized us?" Chris asked when we had stopped shaking. I shook my head.

"I don't think so," I said. "He was probably distracted, looking at the moon."

By then, the eclipse was nearly over, and we sat quietly watching the coppery glow fade. In a few hours, the sun would rise as though the wild night of moon watching and pool hopping had never happened.

"I wish I could take a picture," I said, meaning not just the moon but the whole evening, everything I'd felt and done and seen. "To have something to remember this by."

Chris turned to me then and put his damp hand on my cheek. "Here's something," he said, and he drew my face closer, until I could feel the warmth radiating from his skin. His lips brushed my cheek gently, before I turned my face toward him and kissed him.

Chris lingered in our front yard long after the eclipse was over, at least a half hour after he'd first said he had to leave. I didn't exactly encourage him to go, either. Kissing had made us both lazy. We sat quietly on the grass, holding hands and talking, totally unaware of what time it was.

Finally, we retrieved Chris's bike from the bushes and wheeled it slowly to the street. Together, we folded the damp blanket and stuffed it into the basket. We took our time tying the bundle to the handlebars. I knew that we both wanted to make this magical night last.

"Amy," Chris whispered, placing his hands on the back of my neck, letting his fingers weave through my hair. "I wish I could stay here with you." His lips met mine as surely as if he'd memorized a map of my face. And that last kiss, long and deep, told me everything: that he'd written my name in his notebook, that he'd been dreaming about this moment, as I had, for a very long time.

Reluctantly, we pulled away from each other, and Chris walked me to my window. Quietly, I slid up the screen and pulled myself over the sill.

"I wish . . ." Chris began, but I shushed him. I didn't want him to wake Mom. I leaned out the window and put my lips next to his ear. "See you in physics on Monday," I whispered.

It was already three thirty in the morning when I climbed back through my bedroom window and crawled into my bed. I was relieved to find the apartment dark and quiet, the air still perfumed with apple pie.

In my room, my books were lined up on the white pine shelf, along with the dolphins—plastic, ceramic, and crystal—I'd collected since I was a little girl. On my desk was a bag of m&m's I'd been eating while studying, my physics book,

Matter and Motion, the unopened books for our health project, and a multicolored bundle of ball-point pens.

Everything was just the same as I'd left it, the same as it had always been. But as I changed into a long nightshirt, then climbed into bed, I felt like a different person. I felt as if I'd just returned from a trip around the world. I lay there with my heart racing, thinking, *This is what it feels like when you fall in love.*

Chapter Eight

Blythe got home early from Payson on Sunday. She was so eager to discuss the affairs of my heart that she rushed over to my house immediately. "What happened last night?" she burst out loudly when I opened the kitchen door.

"Shhh," I said, pointing toward the living room, where my mom was reading the paper. I stifled a yawn.

"Hi," Blythe called cheerfully to my mother. "Do you mind if Amy makes a quick trip to the mall with me? There's something I need to pick up."

I looked at Blythe in amazement. She had made that up on the spot, just to get me out of the house so she could hear my story.

Mom looked up from her paper and smiled. "Sure. Have fun, girls."

"Spill it," Blythe said as I climbed into her Jeep. But I wasn't going to give up my secret so easily.

"What do you mean?" I asked innocently. "I'm not doing your homework for you just because you slept through the eclipse."

"I'm not talking about the physics assignment, and you know it," Blythe said, turning the key in the ignition, "I'm talking about your *extracurricular* activities." She backed the Jeep out of our driveway and took off like a maniac. Her boldness was part of what made her a great writer—but it also made her a terror behind the wheel.

She accelerated around a corner. "Blythe, slow down!" I yelled. "I'm too busy fearing for my life to tell you anything."

"Spoilsport," Blythe pouted. But wanting the story, she slowed.

"The eclipse was amazing," I told her.

"I know—I saw it."

"You did?"

"Of course," she said impatiently. "I watched it from Payson."

It seemed impossible to me that we had witnessed the same moon. "What happened after?" Blythe teased me as she cut between two cars. "And don't tell me that after you looked at the moon together, you cuddled up for an exciting game of chess."

"Very funny," I said. "As a matter of fact, we went for a swim."

"Skinny-dipping?" she asked.

"Blythe, don't start rumors," I said. "Of course we kept our clothes on! We went down the street and hopped Joey Favata's pool."

"What possessed you?" She laughed, delighted because it was the kind of thing she would do. "The water must have been freezing."

"It was."

"That's real romantic," she said, rolling her eyes. "Did he kiss you in the Favatas' backyard?"

"Nope," I said. Blythe looked disappointed. "We kissed on the rooftop, and then again in front of the Palms."

Blythe smacked the car seat and whipped her head around. "So you *did* kiss him!" she said. "I knew it! I could just tell!" She sighed dramatically. "A rooftop kiss. That sounds *so* romantic."

"Yeah," I said, unable to wipe a big silly smile off my face.

"Wow," Blythe said. "So . . . is he a good kisser?"

"Awesome," I said.

"Awesome," Blythe repeated. "Does this mean that you'll go with him to the junior-senior dance?"

"I hadn't thought about it," I answered casually, although the mental image of Chris and me dancing together made my pulse race. "It's too far away."

"Let's look at dresses anyway," Blythe said, swinging into the parking lot of the Ocotillo Mall. Even though it had just opened at eleven, the lot was filling up. "You never know how things will turn out." She was going so fast around the turn I swear she left tire treads in the hot asphalt.

"I—I don't know," I began to protest. "I have so much homework to do. I have a physics test on Tuesday and I haven't done any calculus in three days, and I—"

"Amy, *come on*," Blythe said impatiently, pulling the Jeep into a parking space and jerking to a stop. "You have spent your entire life doing your homework. It's time to live a little."

"But I—I just—"

Blythe cut the engine and dropped her keys in her purse. She looked in the rearview mirror, running her fingers through her long hair. "Let's try Buttocks first," she suggested, calling the store by the nickname that had stuck ever since some prankster with a can of spray paint had crossed the two L's.

I tagged behind obediently, trying not to think about how many calculus problems would be waiting for me when I got home. *Live a little,* I ordered myself.

In Bullocks, we were bombarded with a blast of air-conditioning and the buy-me scent of brand-new clothes. We breezed through Shoes and then Cosmetics, dodging the heavily made-up women who offered makeovers and sample spritzes of cologne. "We're on a mission," Blythe called out to a particularly insistent salesperson, as we boarded the escalator bound for the evening-dress department. "We don't have time for avocado facials."

The department was called Cotillion, after the debutante ball the daughters of Phoenix's rich families were presented at every spring. Blythe was quite at home there—after all, she'd been invited (though she'd refused) to join the Desert Debs. I admired the way she strode through this very expensive, very formal department in her combat boots, her long floral skirt, and her tank top. She stopped and held up one dress, then another. She didn't need to look at price tags, but I did. And every time I turned one over, I gasped.

"Three hundred dollars!" I exclaimed, holding up a demure black velvet dress.

"Kind of conservative," Blythe said, squinting. "But it would look all right with a pair of army boots." She took the dress from me and followed a pinch-nosed clerk into the dressing room.

It's weird how all that taffeta and satin and velvet can confuse you.

Finally, I chose a slinky slip dress in bright red— not something that I'd wear in my wildest dreams. Blythe and I came sheepishly out of our cubicles and stood together in front of a large full-length, three-panel mirror. To be honest, we looked like a pair of wannabe actresses auditioning for the wrong parts.

"Do I look like the Bride of Frankenstein?" Blythe asked me, turning carefully in the black velvet dress.

"Not exactly, girlfriend. You look more like the Bride of Rick Finnegan."

Blythe laughed. "Yeah, right," she said, then stared at me. "And you look like you should be riding on a fire truck with a cute fireman."

I laughed. "It is the color of a fire engine."

"It looks gorgeous with your hair," Blythe added.

Blythe pulled her own hair back into a ponytail, then smoothed it and twisted it into an elegant chignon. She looked older and very sophisticated. "I think I like the 'Finnegan,' dress," she said, "even though it isn't quite my style."

"I know what you mean," I said, referring to myself.

Though I never would have picked the red dress before Friday, the longer I wore it, the more I liked the way it looked. The dress was bold and risky, the kind that would encourage a good girl to behave like a wild thing. I whirled before the mirror, remembering how it felt to have Chris's lips on mine.

Then I snapped back to reality. "But it's way too expensive," I said regretfully, smoothing the silky fabric. "I don't spend this much on clothing all year."

"The dance isn't for another month," Blythe reminded me. "We could stake out that dress between now and then, watch to see when it goes on sale."

"Maybe," I said doubtfully, since Blythe and I had vastly different ideas of what was affordable. "In the meantime," I told her, "I've got to get this off before I lose all my willpower and put it on lay-away."

Just then, the salesperson walked over to us. "How are you young ladies doing?" she asked in that fake-sweet tone salespeople always use to show you that they care.

"I'm going to have to pass on Fire Engine," I told her. "How about you, Blythe? Are you going to go for 'Finnegan'?"

The clerk stood there smiling stiffly, trying hard to be amused. She relaxed a bit when Blythe said, "Charge it," and flashed her parents' Visa card. Smiling her approval, the clerk hurried away with the credit card before Blythe could change her mind.

"So," I said to Blythe, trying to sound casual, "I guess this means you'll ask Rick. You look too good in that dress to waste it."

Blythe gazed at me in the mirror, a rare flash of uncertainty in her eyes. "But Rick is . . . our buddy. It's always been the three of us, friends forever. Now it's like everything is changing. What if he doesn't feel the same way I do, what if . . ." She shrugged helplessly. "I don't want to blow our friendship, Amy. Once you've started something like that, you can never go back."

I stared at myself in the sexy red dress, remembering Rick's hurried kiss and all that had happened since: the awkwardness that had replaced my easy friendship with Rick, the thrilling and confusing feelings I had for Chris.

You couldn't go back. That was true. You couldn't stop the planet from spinning, day from turning into night. You couldn't take back a kiss.

"Things are going to change. There's no way of stopping it," I said, more to myself than to Blythe.

Chapter Nine

"YOU'RE SURE IN a good mood," Mom said suspiciously when I offered to wash the Honda before she left for work.

"It's just that it's so gorgeous outside," I said, while his name—*Chris, Chris, Chris*—surged through my brain. After spending the last hour staring at my physics book and daydreaming about Chris, I'd thought of a great way to do something productive *and* daydream about Chris at the same time—wash the car. Besides, I wanted to be alone where I could think about him without worrying that my smile or my mood would betray me. "I can't stand staying inside."

Mom squirted some detergent into a bucket and handed me a sponge. "Can you finish in half an hour? I'm going to take a shower now and get ready for El Rancho."

"No problem," I said, tossing the sponge aside and running to my room to change.

Outside, it was what people call Indian summer. In Phoenix it lasts almost the whole autumn, a stretch of amazing bright-skied, eighty-five-degree days. On such a day, anything seemed possible—breaking a state swimming record, getting a college scholarship, even living happily ever after with a guy like Chris.

I used the garden hose to fill the bucket with sun-warmed water and started sudsing down the car. As I slopped the sponge around on the hood, I wondered where Chris was at that moment and whether or not he was thinking of me.

Our yard was haunted with reminders of the previous night: the rooftop we'd used as a diving board, the lawn where we'd huddled under the blanket and kissed, the bent branches of the oleanders where we'd stashed his bike. Everywhere I looked, I saw Chris's face. For a minute, I thought I must be going crazy, because as I was hosing the suds off the car, I heard his voice too—calling my name.

"Amy!"

I whirled around, expecting a phantom. But instead there he was—riding his bike, dressed for some reason in a linen jacket and a tie. Chris

Shepherd, in the flesh. I was so surprised, I nearly doused him with the garden hose.

"I was hoping you'd be here," he said, dismounting from his bike as he coasted to a stop, his scuffed loafers slapping the puddle of water under his feet. "I don't have your phone number. And I couldn't find it in the book."

"My mom goes by her maiden name," I said. I looked down at my cutoffs and tank top and suddenly felt self-conscious. "It's confusing. She's a Turner. I'm a Wyse."

He barely let me finish. "I had to see you," he said, letting the bike fall, rattling, onto the soaking grass. He put his hand on my shoulder as though he would kiss me right there in broad daylight. I felt the hair on the back of my neck stand on end, both from pleasure and from a sense of danger.

That's when Mom appeared in the back doorway, carrying a bag of trash and wearing her red-and-white checked El Rancho uniform. "Amy, I'm heading off—" she began, then stopped herself midword. "Oh! I didn't know you had company," she said, coughing and clearing her throat several times, the way she did when she disapproved.

"Hi, Mom," I said, quickly pushing his hand from my shoulders. "Chris, this is my mother. Mom, this is Chris Shepherd."

I was ashamed of myself for being embarrassed,

but I couldn't help seeing her grocery store uniform through Chris's eyes. But Chris didn't seem to notice what she was wearing. "Ms. Turner," he said politely, offering his hand. "I'm very pleased to meet you."

Mom shook his hand with her free one. "I'm pleased to meet you too. Excuse me while I go and dump this trash. I'll be right back."

I could tell that Chris was waiting for my mom to say she had heard so much about him. But she wouldn't because I'd kept our stargazing session a secret—in fact, I still hadn't mentioned him at all. "I'm on the Dolphins," Chris said, trying to jog her memory when she returned. "And I'm in Amy's physics class."

Mom didn't respond to this information—she was too busy sizing him up. I guessed the blazer and tie were meant to impress her. "Ms. Turner, may I study with Amy this evening?" he asked, as sweetly as a boy in a 1950s movie. "We have a big physics test on Tuesday." That was all it took for me to be thoroughly charmed.

Charming Mom, though, was considerably harder—she crossed her arms and stood like a guard at the back door. "Would you excuse me a moment?" she asked Chris. "I need to talk to my daughter."

"Of course," he said, as she pulled me aside.

"Who is this young man?" she asked in a whisper. "How come you've never mentioned him before?"

"It—it just happened," I stammered. Wrong choice of words.

"*What* just happened?" Mom asked, her whisper rising.

"Nothing," I said, glancing back at Chris. "I mean, I've known him for a while, but until now, we've never, you know, hung out."

"Amy," Mom reprimanded, "you're not being very articulate." She was quiet for a moment. "I guess there's no harm in studying," she said finally. "Your friend can stay until ten o'clock."

I wasn't sure whether to feel frightened or elated. Had Mom really agreed to leave me alone in the house with a boy she'd just met?

"Thanks, Mom," I said, struggling to be casual. I was afraid I'd seem too eager if I turned around and gave the thumbs-up sign to Chris.

Then, right in front of Chris, Mom kissed my cheek. "Behave yourself, sweetie," she whispered. "I'm counting on you."

With those words, all the happy recklessness I'd been feeling since Saturday disappeared.

I'm counting on you. I knew exactly what she was counting on. She was counting on my not doing what she had done. Not screwing up over a guy. Seventeen years ago Mom was in the Crossroads Baptist Church when she first saw my

99

dad. It was the organ music making her heart swell and the high-pitched singing of the choir and the fervent nodding of the congregation that did her in, she told me. In an instant her well-laid plans were dashed. Mom and Dad were wed in that same church three months later, when I was already on the way. "You were a love child," Mom had always told me, "a beautiful baby."

But just let some boy act like he might care about me and Mom would shake her head and say, "Don't you believe it. If you take the first fast car that comes along, you'll find yourself traveling the road to mediocrity." I hated it when she said that kind of thing. Just because she had made a mistake didn't mean I would.

Mom eyed Chris suspiciously once more before she got into the car. "There's a meat loaf in the oven," she informed us, and then added for Chris's benefit, "Study hard, you two. I'll be home just after ten."

As we waved good-bye to Mom from our walk-way, Chris was already loosening his tie. The knot was flying at half-mast when he went to empty the bucket of sudsy water onto the grass. The tie was swinging loosely from his shoulders by the time we got to the front door.

"You know, the jacket and tie were nice touches," I teased him, "but if you really wanted to impress my mom with your scholarly intentions, you might have at least remembered to bring along your books."

Chris slapped his pants pockets a few times, as though the ten-pound physics tome, *Matter and Motion*, could be crammed in there. "I knew I forgot something," he said with a lopsided, completely irresistible smile.

"That's okay," I said, laughing as I led him into the apartment to our combination living/dining area. "I've got my book. We can share."

It was one thing to be alone with Chris on the rooftop, but a different thing altogether to let him into our apartment. I felt as though my life had been opened up right there in front of him and that everything from my two-person family had been set out on display.

"How about some music?" I asked, hoping noise would somehow soothe me, help me feel more at home in my own house.

"Sure, why not?" said Chris, who had zeroed in on our bookshelves, scanning the rows of colored spines before he selected a book.

I tuned the radio to Mom's classical station because it seemed like the kind of music to go with dinner, even if dinner was only meat loaf. Then, while Chris was still browsing, I searched the hutch for the nice tablecloth we used on holidays, hoping to substitute it for the plastic place mats we normally used. I found it, and I also took out the matching napkins. There were some candles—two were the same dark-green color, but no two were the same size. I snapped three inches off the bottom of the longest one, and held them up together to see if they'd match.

Chris looked up from a book. "You can tell a lot about people by the kinds of books they have," he said.

"Oh? And what does your investigation reveal about me?"

"That you're more practical than romantic," he said. "You've got all these books on science and history, hardly any novels."

"Those are mostly my mom's books," I said quickly. "I've got others in my room." I didn't want him thinking I was some passionless robot, especially when, at that very moment, my heart was shouting out his name between beats.

I set the candles in brass holders and placed them on the table. From the kitchen, I brought two wineglasses and a jumbo bottle of lime seltzer. "I'll get the silverware," Chris offered, "if you'll tell me where it is."

"Top left-hand drawer," I told him, standing back to admire how pretty the table looked.

After we'd brought in our plates of salad and meat loaf, Chris pulled my chair out for me. He'd been raised with manners, that was for sure, because he waited until I'd swallowed my first mouthful before he even took a bite. If my glass was half full, Chris rushed to fill it. And though this attention made me nervous, it was also incredibly romantic.

It was different from the night before, though. Then, we'd talked for hours, blurting out almost anything that came into our heads. Now we were much quieter. Chris had this gentle, sweet expression. When he looked at me and smiled, I felt smart and pretty and cherished and safe. It was a wonderful feeling.

"That was delicious," Chris said, scraping up the last of his second helping. The way he went on about the meat loaf, you'd have thought I'd just served him a Thanksgiving Day feast.

"It's just meat loaf," I said, thinking his family probably ate different things, sophisticated dishes I've never heard of. "Maybe I could copy the recipe. I really like to cook, but my parents' favorite recipe is call-in/take-out," Chris said. I was so surprised I almost laughed.

After dinner, we cleared the dishes, and I took out my physics book. But when I turned to the chapter I'd attempted to review that morning, the words seemed printed in a foreign language. "I don't remember reading this," I said, trying not to panic. Mr. Tayerle was going to test us on the entire astronomy section on Tuesday.

Chris had been sketching in my notebook—

he'd drawn a profile of my face—but he looked up when I said that.

"I've got to reread the whole section," I said, flipping frantically back through the pages, figuring the task was going to take me at least a couple of hours. "I mean, do you even remember when Copernicus published his theory of the universe, or how many miles there are between the Earth and the moon?"

"It was 1543," Chris answered, going back to his drawing. "And the distance between the Earth and the moon is two hundred thirty-nine thousand miles. There are ninety-three million miles between the Earth and the sun."

His casual confidence only made me feel more shaky. "You must have a photographic memory," I said.

"I guess I do," Chris answered. He kept sketching my face, shading in the contours of my high cheekbones, drawing in dark eyebrows above my eyes. "For instance, Amy, when I shut my eyes, all I see is you."

He took my hand then, and kissed the palm. Then he kissed my wrist and up my arm—sweet little feathery kisses—before I reluctantly pulled away.

I'm counting on you. My mother's words were ringing so clearly in my head, she might as well have been in the same room with us. "Chris," I said, hoping my voice sounded steady, "I have to study."

"Want me to quiz you?" he asked.

"No, thanks," I said, staring miserably at the incomprehensible graphs and tables in the book. I could just picture my mom's face when I told her I got a *D* on my physics test. I had let things slip, I really had. Just a few days of slacking off could turn everything around for me. "If you don't mind, I'm going to re-read a few chapters on my own."

"Okay. I'll just draw, then," he said.

I hesitated. He was making this tough. "I—I meant, I need to study alone."

"You want me to leave?" he asked, a hurt expression on his face.

"Chris, I don't *want* you to, but I can't study when you're around."

He stood up and smiled. "Okay. I'll see you tomorrow." He held out his hand. "Walk me to the door?"

"Sure," I said, standing and taking his hand.

Walking Chris to the door proved to be disastrous to my study time. An hour later we were still kissing and talking and saying good-bye. *I'll just stay up a little later,* I kept telling myself. Finally, I pushed him out the door. "See you in class," I said, trying to sound firm.

Then I went back to studying astronomy. I started the chapter on eclipses and tried to recall the one I'd actually seen, the one we should have taken notes on. But all I could remember were the brownies we'd eaten, and the faint taste of chocolate on Chris's lips when I should have been studying the moon.

I was looking for notepaper in the drawer of my desk when I came across the financial aid form for colleges my counselor, Mr. Hatch, had given me to give to Mom several weeks ago. At the time, I'd hidden it away rather than show it to her—it looked as complicated as income taxes, and I knew she'd have to call my long-lost dad in order to fill it out. If I didn't hang on to my *A* in physics, there was no way I could count on a merit scholarship.

With a feeling of dread, I placed the form on the table, where Mom would be sure to see it when she got home from work.

Mom knocked on my bedroom door at ten fifteen. She opened it and walked in, holding up the financial aid form. "I suppose this means I've got to call your father," she said. "I imagine he still lives in Austin. Unless he's gone off and married some poor woman."

An unmistakable look of pain crossed her face. "You don't have to actually fill it out until next year," I told her quickly, turning around in my desk chair. "My counselor just thought it might be a

106

good idea to get prepared a year ahead."

To my surprise, Mom let out a laugh. "We'd both better hope that your father hasn't struck gold and suddenly become a millionaire," she said.

"Why not, if he could help us?" I asked.

"His added income might hurt us more than it would help," she said wearily, sitting down on my bed. "I'm not sure he'd fork it over, even if he had it. Way back when, your father didn't see the value in my going to college. So I'm not so sure he'd want to treat you to an expensive education at a private school."

"I guess not," I said glumly. While Mom had struggled alone to raise me all these years, my dad had been a shadow in the background, barely more than a tightfisted signature on a yearly birthday card. How could I expect him to help pay for college, when Mom had to get on his case constantly just so he'd send his court-ordered child support? "You don't have to call him if you really don't want to," I said.

Mom was quiet a moment, considering. "If I don't call, we'll never know the answer, and it's better to know before you start applying to schools," she said in a sensible voice. She started to walk out of my room, then turned. "But I must say I'm dreading having to dodge your father's dangerous charm."

I knew my father had swept her off her feet all

those years ago, but I'd never heard her describe him as charming.

"What do you mean?" I asked.

"Your father always had a way of convincing me that he could make anything happen," she said, sighing. "As if love alone is magic—when we both know that in the end you have to rely on yourself."

As she closed my door, I had a sinking feeling that she could just as well have been talking about Chris.

Chapter Ten

"**D**ON'T WORRY. WE'LL go to the library to-night and review the whole astronomy unit," Chris said at lunch on Monday, after I'd spent fifteen minutes telling him how nervous I was about the physics test the next day. "I'll pick you up at seven."

The two of us were sitting face-to-face on the school lawn, squinting in the strong Arizona sun and sharing a bottle of Snapple and a bag of Chee•tos.

"I'm not sure," I said slowly. I knew it was a dangerous idea to see him at all that night. Even at the library.

"Oh, come on, Amy. I promise we'll get a lot done," Chris said. "You can have your own study carrel if you want. You won't even know I'm there—unless you have a physics question you want to ask me."

I looked at his serious, pleading face and laughed.

"Please?" he urged. "There's no way I can go a whole night without seeing your face."

I felt the beat of my heart pick up speed. Those were the kind of words I treasured, that I dreamed about hearing from him. How could I say no?

I pointed an orange Chee•to-stained finger at him. "If you absolutely *promise* to let me study and you *promise* you'll take me home early so we can get some sleep before the swim meet."

"I will," he said happily. "I really will." He tackled me on the lawn and pinned me down for a long kiss.

There could have been teachers passing by right then. Coach August and the entire swim team could have been standing there gaping at us. The principal could have looked out his office window and wondered what in the world had happened to practical, responsible Amy Wyse.

But the kiss felt so perfect I didn't even care.

"First I'm going to read the whole astronomy section over again, from beginning to end," I was telling Chris as we sped along in his mother's Saab to the public library. "Then I'm going to do the—"

"Whoa," Chris said, his eyes focused on a cluster of lights twinkling in the distance. I realized he wasn't paying any attention to me.

"What?" I asked.

Chris suddenly got this really excited look on his face and swung into the left lane.

"What?" I said again. "Where are you going?"

"Amy, this is going to be so cool."

"What's going to be so cool?" I persisted.

Chris hung a left and sped in a direction I was pretty sure wasn't going to get us to the library.

"Quick detour," Chris told me, examining the street signs. "I promise it won't take long, and it will be worth it."

"What could be worth failing my physics test?" I murmured, but Chris was so absorbed in navigation that I don't think he heard me.

"Okay, Amy, get ready." Chris pulled the car into a dark parking lot and practically leapt out. He ran around to my side, opened the door, and grabbed my hand to yank me to my feet. He led me across the parking lot and down a dusty path. "Now, close your eyes," he ordered.

"What?"

"Come on, close 'em."

"Chris, *what* are we doing?" I demanded, but my curiosity was getting the best of me, so I closed my eyes.

He led me along blindly for another twenty yards or so, then stopped. I could hear unfamiliar whirring sounds and faint music in the distance.

"Okay," he said, and I could hear the excitement in his voice, "you can open them."

I did. It took me a second to focus on the blurring chaos of colored lights at the bottom of the hill. It was a carnival. A big, blazing, whirling carnival with a merry-go-round and a Ferris wheel and music and games and people shouting. I felt a tingle of anticipation in the night air. "Wow."

We had approached it from the back, so we had missed the cars and buses and signs at the entrance. We had the magical view all to ourselves.

"Amazing, isn't it?" Chris said.

He grabbed my hand, and we went running all the way down the hill and into the lights. Somewhere in the back of my mind, a voice that sounded a lot like my mom's was reminding me how unprepared I was for my physics test. *Very bad idea,* that voice was telling me. But the bright lights and the music and the electric tingle of Chris's hand wrapped tightly around mine were too intoxicating to resist.

We started with the merry-go-round, two of us clambering onto one horse. Then we bought big blue clouds of cotton candy and spent forever hurling a baseball at a pyramid of cans, hoping to win an enormous purple bear.

By the time we got to the Ferris wheel, we were on a giddy high from sugar and laughter and exertion. But as the wheel carried us slowly to the top, my body began to relax into Chris's. He gently circled my waist with his arm and drew me even closer as we went up and up and up.

I sighed with joy as the lights of Phoenix spread out under us, the air grew still, and the music grew faint. When we reached the very top, the Ferris wheel paused and our little basket swung from side to side. I had that thrilling buzz in my stomach of looking down a long, long way, yet feeling safe at the top.

Chris held me in his arms and kissed me so tenderly that the world stopped and the music stopped and all of my thoughts stopped except for one: that I wanted this moment to last forever.

Chapter Eleven

R EALITY SET IN the next morning.

Ten minutes before physics, I sat outside on the school lawn, still trying in vain to cram facts and figures in. Blythe brought me frosted doughnuts and a Coke from the school snack bar, on the theory that sugar and caffeine would make the information stick.

"I've never seen you like this," she muttered once or twice while watching my agonized face as I hurriedly flipped through the textbook.

When the first bell rang I slammed the book shut on Copernicus and took a big swig of Coke. "We might as well go to physics and get this over with."

Chris's seat was empty. I worried for a moment that he would miss the test, but he burst through the door at the last minute, walked over to my desk, and handed me a bouquet of daisies. "Good luck, Amy," he said with a heart-melting smile. "I'll be thinking of you."

"How about if we try to think of physics?" I suggested, but I couldn't help feeling surprised and charmed by the flowers. And they made me feel hopeful too.

Somehow, when Chris was around, it seemed that anything was possible. Even getting straight *A*'s without studying, or winning that day's meet in spite of a sloppy flip turn. I sat up straighter in my seat and even said thank you when Tayerle passed out the test.

But my hopefulness slowly turned to panic as I read the first question, then the next and the next. I kept skipping questions, trying to find one I could answer. Then, before I knew it, I was halfway down the page. The problem was, Tayerle was asking about patterns and systems and distances, while I'd been fixed on the mysterious movement of the planets and the coppery glow of the eclipse. Clearly, I had learned about astronomy the wrong way. There was absolutely no room on Tayerle's exam for romance.

The hands on the wall clock seemed to spin faster than I could think. Everyone around me was calmly filling in answers, but I was frantically scribbling. When Tayerle said, "Time's up," I tossed down my pencil, half in frustration, half in relief that at least it was over.

"That was tough," I told Blythe afterward.

"Really?" she said, her face registering surprise. "I thought it was a piece of cake."

I suddenly had the sick feeling that I'd really blown it; even my bouquet of daisies couldn't console me. Frustrated, I vowed to swim during my lunch hour, practicing flip turn after flip turn until I got it right. The only way to save the day from total disaster, I decided, was to come in first at that afternoon's meet.

But in the next moment I wavered, when Chris caught up to me outside and gently took my hand. "Are you free for lunch today?" he asked. "I borrowed my mom's car again, and I was thinking we could do our own private carbo load."

I knew I needed the practice time more than I needed a carbo load that day, but I just wanted to be cheered up after the awful morning I'd had. I threw my arms around his neck, surprising Blythe and even Chris with this outburst of affection.

"Yes, please, take me away from all this!" I said, only half joking.

At lunch, Chris and I shared a chimichanga and drank milk shakes in the front seat of his mother's Saab. Outside, rain was threatening, and the clouds looked heavy. "I'm stuffed," I said when

117

we'd finished. "Actually, I don't feel so well."

But it was more than just the chimichanga—it was too many days in a row of staying up late. Just thinking about that health project I hadn't started yet made me feel even more tired. I laid my head back on the car seat and sighed.

"What's wrong?" Chris asked, stroking my hair.

For some reason, I didn't want to admit to him how behind I was, or how badly I'd done on the test. "I'm just thinking about the meet today," I lied. "I hope I can remember how to swim. I didn't get very much sleep after we got home last night."

"Me neither," Chris said, winding a lock of my hair slowly around his closed fist.

"Were you worried about the test?" I asked hopefully. Somehow things would seem better if I knew that Chris had lost sleep over it too.

"Worried about physics?" Chris asked me, as if the idea were absurd. "No, I was just tossing and turning all night, thinking about you."

The meet that day was not my finest hour. Not even close.

"Amy, what's going on with you?" Coach August asked me afterward, pulling me aside as my teammates boarded the bus. "You were third in all your races, and you looked like you were asleep on the starting block. You've got to do better than that." He shook his head. "You're the best

118

freestyler we've got, Amy. We're counting on you."

I winced at his choice of words. "It won't happen again, Coach. I promise. All I need is a good night's sleep."

"Make sure you get one before regionals," he said. "You won't be able to slack off when you're swimming against some of the best swimmers in the state."

I had my head bowed during Coach August's lecture, but I looked up just in time to see Jill Renfrew sitting in the bus, her ear pressed against a half-inch crack in her window. "Hi, Jill," I called out, and I could tell by the way she started that she'd overheard our conversation. She turned to talk to Shannon, pretending not to hear me, but when I got on the bus, she had this smug, knowing smile on her face.

"It's pretty sad," I said as I passed her, "that you're so insecure you have to spy on me."

I must have hit a nerve, because Jill turned around and glared at me as I headed down the aisle. "We'll see who's sad," she threatened as I sat down next to Chris, "when it's me, not you, who swims the hundred free at the regional meet."

"I can't stand this," I muttered, leaning my head on the back of the seat.

Chris, who'd been reading *Science Digest* intently, looked up and smiled. "What?" he said, sounding like a space cadet.

No wonder Chris was such a good student. No wonder he had aced his SATs. He could shut out everything that went on around him when he wanted to.

Unlike me.

"Never mind," I told him quietly. "It's nothing."

Chapter Twelve

ALL CHRIS HAD to do was whisper, "Amy, I have to see you," and I forgot all about the fact that it was a school night or that I had homework. One night we went out for pizza, another night we went to a horror movie, then drank cappuccino at the café in the mall. But most nights we met at midnight on my rooftop.

Phoenix had seen the last of Indian summer, and now the nights were growing cold. To keep warm, I would wait for Chris inside my bedroom, and crawl out the window only when I saw him round the corner on his bike.

Together, we would climb as quietly as we could up to the chilly roof tiles, like two skiers seeking the top of a slope. I always felt as if we were leaving the world of school and friends and the Dolphins behind and ascending into some special place all our own.

Each time we met, Chris brought me something he'd made in his bedroom while he waited for his parents to fall asleep. There was a sketch of me he'd done from memory, a mobile of the universe made from paper clips and notebook paper, a card with my name "embroidered" on the front of it in multicolored felt pens. Once, he left behind a baseball cap, and that was my most treasured gift. The hat was worn in places, and I could smell the soapy scent of his hair in the brim. For nearly a week, I slept with the hat tucked beneath my pillow before I reluctantly gave it back.

But one night about three weeks after we had first climbed to the roof, Chris showed up with something that wasn't homemade. "Amy, I want you to have this," he said, and he handed me a tiny box wrapped in department store paper.

I was sure I knew what it was before I even opened it, but I couldn't quite believe I was right. I mean, guys didn't give girls rings anymore, at least as far as I knew. Maybe someone Mom's age might have worn a boy's ring in high school, but among my friends, "going steady" hadn't been cool since about the seventh grade.

I tried to look surprised as I tore off the wrapping paper and cracked the hinged lid. And then I really was surprised, because what lay there on the box's velvet lining wasn't a ring after all, but a small, brass key.

It wasn't a modern key, like the kind you'd use to open your front door. It was old, small, intricate, and slightly worn. "The key to your heart?" I teased Chris as I examined it, turning the key over in my hand.

"You could say that," he answered. "It opens a locker full of treasures I used to have, this old sea chest I got from my grandpa."

"What was in it?" I asked, imagining yellowed pirate maps and gold doubloons.

"Old toys and models, mostly," Chris explained. "Souvenirs from being a kid. But when we moved into our new house, my parents must have gotten rid of it. They swear they stored it in the garage, but I haven't seen it since."

"That's so sad," I whispered, thinking of my collection of dolphins, and the stained and scruffy animals who lived in my closet, piled cozily in an old doll cradle. I hadn't played with them since I was a little girl, but I wouldn't dream of giving them up.

Chris shrugged. "Mom said she wanted to start over in our brand-new house."

"But they're like old friends," I protested. "You can't just decide one day to toss them out."

Chris took my hand and held it, so that the key was pressed between our palms. "I hope I'll have

123

you forever," he said, and I understood then that the key meant not what he had lost but what we would have together.

"You do," I said. "You will."

Later, when Chris helped me back through my window, I briefly thought about how fast my life was moving—faster than I knew how to handle. My days blurred together—one long run of school, swim practice, and evenings spent falling asleep over homework, then waking up and climbing out the window to see Chris. Our secret meetings—we called them the Astronomy Club—were the only parts of the day I looked forward to. I wasn't swimming well, and I was behind in my classes.

I can't explain why we didn't go on more normal dates. Partly, I knew my mom would not let me date anyone on a regular basis, but mostly it was because it was so romantic, climbing up to my roof and looking at stars and having our own secret place.

"I don't want to go in," I said that night, hating to say good-bye.

"In that case," Chris teased me, "why don't you invite me in out of the cold?" He leaned forward through the open window to kiss me.

"I can't," I said, meaning I couldn't invite him in, not that I couldn't kiss him.

Just then, my door slowly creaked open, and we both heard Mom's angry gasp. There we were, the two of us, caught in the hall light. Mom was silhouetted in the doorway, and she was furious.

"Amy, what are you doing!" she demanded. "Who's there with you? Do you have any idea what time it is?" She lobbed her questions at me so quickly that I barely had time to react.

"Ms. Wyse—I mean Turner—it's my fault," Chris said, trying to defend me. "I knocked on Amy's window. She was just this minute pleading with me to go home."

Mom marched over to the window. Her lips tightened with anger. "You'd better get home," she told Chris. "If this happens again, I'll call your parents," she warned before slamming the window shut. I could feel myself trembling—with fear and anger—when Mom whirled around.

"I can't believe you did that!" I screamed at her. "We weren't doing anything wrong!" My hand sought the cover of my jeans pocket and my fingers wrapped protectively around the key Chris had given me. "Besides," I added, holding back tears, "I can take care of myself!"

"Amy, what has gotten into you? Do you call staying up until all hours on a school night taking care of yourself?"

"I can handle it," I said, more quietly that time because I wasn't so sure I could. I was thinking of the C I'd gotten on the physics test, the health and English books I'd only skimmed, and the other homework I hadn't even started.

"I know you think you can," Mom told me. "But for the time being, you're grounded. You're to be in bed by ten on school nights, and to come straight home after school or swimming practice."

"That's not fair," I protested. "You can't ground me anyway. I'm almost seventeen."

Mom stormed out into the hallway. "Maybe this will remind you," she told me, "that you're not quite grown up yet."

Chapter Thirteen

T HE NEXT DAY, I strung the key on a satin cord and wore it like a piece of expensive jewelry around my neck. I was hoping it would glitter defiantly in the sunlight, but unfortunately, the day was overcast.

"What's that? A cross?" Jill asked me at practice. We were doing timed trials for the meet the next day, and I guess she was worried that I might gain an edge on the competition by appealing to a higher, holy source.

"It's a key," I told her, covering it with my palm. The metal was cold. "I got it from Chris."

"What a weird gift! You're not going to wear that in the pool, are you?" Jill asked, pushing her straight brown hair underneath her swimming cap.

The truth was, I hadn't been planning to—I was

afraid the chlorine in the water might turn the brass green. But when Jill asked me, I felt I had to, just to spite her. We were the last two people in the locker room, and I headed toward the door. "Sure, why not?" I called back.

Once in the water, I discovered that the key lay against my body neatly as long as I kept moving forward, but it bobbed around in the water whenever I turned. Twice, the key rapped me on the forehead when I was upside-down underwater. Finally, on my fourth flip turn, the cord and the key wriggled free from my neck.

I stopped traffic in the swim lane as I dog-paddled in place, trying to find my treasure. "What's your problem?" Jill asked as she swam up beside me. She had an I-told-you-so grin on her face.

Usually I tried to be cool with her. But I was too tired today. *You're the problem*, I was thinking. And let me tell you, one second longer and the words would have sprung from my lips.

But just then I looked up and saw Chris standing at the edge of the pool, watching me. I knew he must have seen what had just happened. "There's no problem," I told Jill, as I watched him dive purposefully into the water.

"Looking for this?" he asked me, smiling, as he emerged a moment later holding my key.

"Yes! Thank you," I said. I stood in the water while he knotted the cord tighter and slipped it around my neck. Behind me, he leaned close so that Jill couldn't hear. "I hope you didn't get in too much trouble, Amy," he whispered. "I didn't want to leave you last night, the way your mom was yelling."

"It was all right," I told him, trying to sound bold—bolder than I felt. "I told her that we hadn't done anything wrong and that I could take care of myself."

"How'd she take it?" Chris asked, his eyes full of concern.

What I said next was only half true. "She just wants me to be careful."

Just then Coach August blew his whistle to organize us for timed trials. All week, he'd been taking notes on his clipboard, trying to decide which Dolphins would swim in the qualifying meet. Usually, I was the undisputed choice for the 100-meter freestyle, but that day, Coach called my name and asked me to join Jill at the other end of the pool.

"I can't believe he's making me race her," I said to Chris under my breath.

"Just relax and remember your flip turn," Chris said, patting me on the shoulder. "He's probably just doing it to shake you up."

If that was Coach August's intention, he didn't have to shake hard. I was already shaking as I got out of the water and walked what felt like a hundred miles around the pool's perimeter to the starting block.

"Hurry up, Amy," Jill said, shaking out her arms and legs as if she'd been waiting all day.

"I'll be telling you that in the water," I said, "while I'm waiting for you to catch up."

But when the starting buzzer sounded, my foot slipped and I left the block a split second behind. When I entered the water, I was flailing, and it took me at least a lap and a half to hit my stride. By the third length, I was sailing—everything depended on my final flip turn. "Don't hit it, don't hit it, don't hit it," I chanted from habit, forgetting what Chris had taught me. "Don't hit it, don't hit it, don't hit it . . ." *WHACK!*

As I finished the last lap, I was sure that I'd swum my very worst time. I slapped the pool deck and jerked my neck around to see where Jill was in the pool. "I'm here, Amy," she said smugly, and I realized that she was already out of the water, resting, her feet dangling into the pool.

"It's like she's waiting for me to blow it," I fumed to Chris after practice, "so she can take my place at regionals."

"Don't let her get to you," Chris urged, as I waited with him at the bus stop. My bus always came about ten minutes after his.

"I can't help it," I said. "She made me so self-conscious today, I couldn't do one decent turn. Which is not the way I want to feel the day before a meet." Even as I was saying it, I knew Jill wasn't really the one to blame. I was.

Chris's bus roared as it turned the corner onto Central. It was rush hour, and through the windows I could see that all the seats were filled with downtown workers, people who I imagined were going home to pretty houses with heated swimming pools.

"Amy, come home with me," Chris said, as the bus pulled to a stop at the curb. "We can grab a bite to eat and study, and you can practice your turn in our pool."

I thought fleetingly of the health project that was due at the end of the week. Blythe had done a survey in the *Thunder* of students' views on everything from love to marriage to romantic movies. She'd already collected responses from two hundred kids and tallied the results. All I had to do, she kept reminding me, was read the books she'd checked out of the library and write up an analysis of the survey.

I knew by then that studying with Chris was asking for academic disaster. After the night of the carnival, we'd gone to the library a few times together after school, and he'd do things like write love notes in the margins of my composition book or try to kiss me while I was trying to read. I could just imagine what he'd do when he learned the topic of my homework was intimacy!

But on the other hand, I did need to practice swimming. Otherwise, I'd probably try to turn in the lane tomorrow and end up somewhere near Timbuktu.

"You kids on or off?" barked the bus driver.

"On," I said suddenly, skipping up the metal stairs. In the end, it wasn't worry about my flip turn that tipped the scales toward going home with Chris. To be honest, I just wanted to spend time with him, to feel his arms around me, his cheek brush against mine, the gentle searching of his lips.

Of course, I didn't tell him I was grounded—I didn't want Chris to think I was a little kid.

"Don't worry, Amy, everything'll work out," he said, smiling.

"Practice makes perfect," I said with a shrug.

The Shepherds lived in a neighborhood of grand, expensive houses. Their home was a two-story, Tudor-style stucco, with a Bermuda-grass lawn twice the size of the courtyard in our apartment complex, and a giant, three-car garage. I couldn't help admiring this easy abundance, but it also made me kind of mad. I thought about how my mom had to work two jobs just to pay the bills.

"It's very nice," I said as we stood in the cavernous entryway. Chris deprogrammed the burglar alarm and hung up his house key.

"Thanks. I liked our old house better," he said, leading me through an immaculate white kitchen, which was the same size as our living room. He slid open a glass door that led onto the patio. "But this house does have a pretty good pool."

He wasn't kidding. The pool was incredible: Olympic-sized and heated, with wisps of fog rising from its surface. I bent down to test the water with my fingertips and found it warmer than the early-evening air. "If I didn't know you had a burglar alarm," I teased Chris, "I might just climb your fence and hop your pool."

"Be my guest," Chris said, grinning. Then he grabbed my hand and started pulling me toward the deep end with him.

"Chris, don't even think about it," I warned him as he dragged me along. "Chris, you better not—Chris—"

Splash! He threw me into the water, fully clothed and shrieking.

"Just think how light you'll feel when you race tomorrow if you practice tonight wearing twenty pounds of wet clothes," he said, laughing from the side of the pool as I flailed around heavily in the water.

He was trying to be funny, but he was making me mad. It was more than the fact that he'd ruined my outfit, a hand-knit sweater and black jeans whose labels screamed, DRY CLEAN ONLY and NO BLEACH. And it was more than the fact that I was going to have to wear my soggy black sneakers home.

It had suddenly occurred to me that before we were a couple, he'd taken my flip-turn problem seriously. Now he was making fun of me. Maybe it was because he suspected I hadn't come home with him to rehearse my turn for tomorrow but to practice the delicate art of the kiss. Even if it was true, which it partly was, I didn't want him thinking that.

"How am I supposed to practice turning?" I asked irritably, struggling with arms and legs as heavy as tree trunks. "I can barely move!"

He was still laughing, and I was getting madder and madder.

"Chris, stop it!" I finally exploded. "It's not a joke. This is a good sweater—and now it's ruined. And I really do need to practice!"

When Chris saw the anger in my face, his smile disappeared. "I'm sorry," he said. He took off his shirt and jumped in. "I only wanted to make you laugh. I'll buy you another sweater," he offered, as he paddled awkwardly toward me.

But the longer I treaded there in my water-logged clothes, the angrier I felt. "It really isn't funny, Chris. What do my clothes matter? If I blow my flip turns tomorrow, I might not get to swim at regionals. And if I don't swim at regionals, there's no way I'll be considered for a swimming scholarship next year." I felt tears filling my eyes. "Maybe if I had plenty of money for college the way you do, it wouldn't matter so much," I said quietly. "But I don't."

"Come on, Amy," he pleaded, as I swam-dragged myself away from him and toward the pool edge. "I didn't mean anything by it."

When I got to the metal stepladder, I began to pull myself up and out. But that's when I realized the air outside was about twenty degrees colder than the water in the pool. "How am I going to get home now?" I asked in a voice fringed with tears, collapsing back in the water. "I—I can't take the bus in these clothes—I'll freeze to death."

"I'll drive you there when my parents get home," Chris promised. "In the meantime, wait here." I didn't exactly have a choice, so I kept on treading water while he hoisted himself out of the pool and hurried across the patio, tracking water into the house.

He hurried back out a moment later carrying a big towel and an armload of dry clothes. "You can change into these in the pool house," he said, unfurling a pair of Dolphins sweatpants, dry athletic socks, and a plaid flannel shirt. He put the clothes on a lounge chair and held the towel out to me like a blanket, welcoming me into its warmth.

"Amy, I really am sorry," he whispered a few minutes later when I came out of the pool house, dry and dressed in his clothes. He had changed too in the meantime, and was dressed in a nearly identical outfit.

"Forget it," I said, although I couldn't forget it. The plunge into the pool was like a slap in the face that brought me back to reality. I moved away from him. "I really do have to go home now," I told him, glancing at my luckily waterproof watch. "I've got a lot of homework."

"Okay." He put his arms around me and kissed my forehead. "Let me just grab the keys from my mom, and I'll take you."

I gulped. "You mean your mom is home?" I spun around and saw Mrs. Shepherd standing there on the patio, elegant and perfectly groomed in a beige suit.

"Hello. You must be Amy," she said warmly. I could tell by her fixed smile how hard she was trying not to notice that Chris and I had just been embracing. Not to mention the fact that I was dressed head to toe in her son's clothes.

"Uh, h-hi, Mrs. Shepherd. It's nice to meet you," I stammered. I'd seen her at swim meets a few times, but we'd never been introduced. "Chris and I were going to practice flip turns, but then he pushed me in. . . ." I stopped myself just short of a full confession. I didn't like the way I sounded.

136

Mrs. Shepherd laughed, but I had this sinking feeling that she didn't believe me.

Chris, the real culprit, seemed totally unfazed. I waited in silence for him to explain to her what had really happened, but he didn't.

"I'm taking Amy home now" was all he said, holding out his palm to receive her car keys.

"Don't bother—I'm getting my things, and I'll take the bus," I said quietly. I stormed back to the pool house, stuffed my wet clothes into my gym bag, put on my soggy sneakers, then stormed out. I half expected him to be waiting, but he was nowhere in sight.

As I walked to the bus stop, I kept thinking Chris would follow and try to stop me, but he didn't. Even though I'd refused a ride from him, I couldn't help but feel that *he'd* abandoned *me*.

As I stood waiting at the bus stop, looking out into the lonely street, I wondered if I had over-reacted. Maybe I'd blown it with Chris the same way I'd blown my flip turn. Fear made me pull away from him and turn too early, the way it did when I reached the pool wall.

Finally, the bus pulled up. With tears in my eyes, I paid the driver, took a seat in the back, and stared out the window into the darkness all the way home.

Chapter Fourteen

SINCE MOM USUALLY works evenings, I was surprised to see the lights on in the apartment and the Honda parked out in front. "Where have you been?" she asked when I came in through the back door and dropped my gym bag and backpack on the floor. She stood in front of the dinner table, which was set for two. "It's almost seven thirty, young lady, and you're supposed to be grounded."

"I thought you were at El Rancho," I said, caught completely off guard.

"I took the night off," she answered, pouring herself some iced tea. "And what in the world are you wearing?"

"You wouldn't understand," I told her, arms crossed in front of me. "It's too hard to explain."

"I'm an intelligent person," Mom said. "Why don't you try me?"

She motioned for me to sit down. It would have been easier if she'd just yelled at me—at least then I could storm off to my room. Instead, she'd made this dinner as a peace offering, and had waited for hours for me to come home. It made me feel guilty, and feeling guilty always made me act defensively.

"Okay, I was at Chris's," I said, trying to provoke her. She just sat there quietly, waiting for me to go on. So I told her how Jill Renfrew had acted at practice and how important it was for me to do well in the next meet so I would make regionals.

"I didn't mean to disobey you," I said awkwardly. "It's just that Chris offered to help with my flip turn."

"So what's with the boy's clothes?" Mom interrupted.

"Chris pushed me into his pool," I said, then quickly added, "He was trying to be funny. He didn't mean anything bad."

"Oh, Amy." She sighed. I thought she would be angry at me all over again, but instead she put down her fork, reached out, and gently stroked my cheek. I realized when she touched me that what had seemed like meanness the night before was actually real concern. But then she ruined everything by saying, "I'm afraid this Chris is bad news."

"No, he's not," I said defensively.

The problem seemed so obvious to me right then. If I lived my life the way I wanted to, I couldn't please my mom. It was impossible. But if I did everything she wanted, then *I'd* be unhappy.

"Amy, I don't want to argue," Mom said, sounding weary.

"You wouldn't say that," I told her, "if you really knew him."

Just then, to my relief, the phone rang.

"Has he called you yet?" Blythe blurted out as soon as I'd answered the phone. I assumed she was talking about Chris.

"Not yet," I told her, keeping my voice low. "I mean, I was just over at his house."

"You were?" Blythe asked, sounding disappointed. "Then you must have said yes."

"Blythe, slow down," I demanded. "I don't know what you're talking about. Said yes to what?"

"What else?" she said, exasperated. "The junior-senior dance."

"Oh, that," I said. "I don't think I'm going. I'm sort of mad at Chris right now."

"Who said anything about Chris?" she said. "Rick told me today that he's going to ask you."

"Rick?" I said, surprised. I guess I was flattered—I mean, it was really sweet of him. But at the same time, it was kind of awkward. He'd hardly talked to me in the past couple of weeks—and I'd barely thought of him. He'd probably heard about me and Chris and felt sorry for me. "Thanks for warning me," I said, trying to be funny. "I'll stay away from him tomorrow and keep the phone off the hook."

Blythe didn't laugh. "If you don't want to go with him, then you should tell him so. It's not fair to him, and it's not fair to me."

I guess the weeks of sneaking out and staying up late really had caught up with me, because I snapped at Blythe in a way she didn't deserve. "Who cares about that stupid dance!" I practically yelled at her, not caring if Mom heard. "Especially since I'm not even going."

When I hung up, Mom just stared at me. "Amy, I'm surprised at you. Is that any way to speak to your best friend?"

I didn't want to talk about it. I didn't want to talk about Blythe or Chris or swimming or anything else. I quickly cleared my dishes and hurried off to my room. "I'll apologize to her tomorrow," I promised. "Right now, I've got too much homework to do."

I started out with the best of intentions. I opened my notebook, sharpened three pencils, and dragged Blythe's stack of student surveys from the floor up to my desk. But it was already nine o'clock by the time I was ready to actually read them, and I was yawning so much I could barely see the pages through my watery eyes. My eyelids started drooping before I'd finished the first survey.

Finally, I gave up and turned out my desk light, telling myself I'd finish later, after I'd had just a few hours' sleep. I set my alarm clock for midnight and collapsed across my bed, with Chris's clothes still on.

When Mom woke me at a quarter to seven the next morning, I realized with horror that I must have turned off my alarm and gone back to sleep. And I was still exhausted. And there was absolutely no way I was going to get the project done.

Mom eyed my strange, rumpled outfit as I stumbled into the bathroom to brush my teeth. "Amy, don't skip breakfast," she reminded me. "Eat something substantial, please, since today's your qualifying meet."

"Oh, yeah," I grumbled around my toothbrush. "I forgot." Mouth foaming with toothpaste, I grabbed my drying bathing suit from the shower rack where I'd hung it the night before, and stuffed it into my Dolphins bag. I went back to brushing my teeth.

I must have looked pretty pitiful, because Mom came up behind me and planted a kiss on the top of my head. "Just ignore that Renfrew girl," she advised me, "because when you think about it, the only person you're competing against is yourself."

"Ummm-mmm," I mumbled. I didn't have the

heart to tell Mom that I wasn't even thinking about the qualifying meet. I had a much bigger problem. In all my years of school, I had never missed the deadline for an assignment. But that day, for the first time, I was going to have to tell Blythe and Ms. Hutchinson that the health project would be late.

Just to give you an idea of how terrible my day was, telling Ms. Hutchinson I'd been delinquent with my project was the high point. I decided to talk to her in the morning, even before I spoke to Blythe. Her response surprised me. "As you know, I'm reluctant to give extensions," she told me, studying me with her intelligent brown eyes. "But Amy, you're such a good student, and up to this point you've done such stellar work, that I'm going to give you an extra week."

"Thank you, Ms. Hutchinson," I said gratefully. "It'll be a much better project." Even though I got exactly what I wanted, I couldn't help but feel like an impostor as I turned and left the room. I knew Ms. Hutchinson had been lenient because of the "good student" label I'd worn proudly since grade school. Would she have been so forgiving if she knew about all the late hours I'd been putting in for the Astronomy Club?

The first terrible shock came in physics. We'd had another test at the beginning of the week, and Mr. Tayerle handed it back today. To my horror, I got a *D*. Next to the red-penned, circled letter, Mr. Tayerle had written, "Amy, what happened?"

I couldn't answer that question, not for Mr. Tayerle or for myself. I wasn't going to admit to anyone that love might have something to do with it. *This won't happen again,* I promised myself, and I turned the paper over and buried it in the back of my book.

When I walked out of physics class, Chris was waiting for me. "Did you get home okay last night?" he asked.

I couldn't believe it. He was acting as if nothing were wrong. "Fine," I said and turned toward my locker.

Like a friendly puppy, Chris followed after me. "So how'd you do on the physics test?"

"I don't want to talk about it," I said, banging my locker open with such force that Chris jumped. I threw my physics book in the locker, grabbed my books for English, then slammed the door shut. "I suppose you aced it," I snapped.

Chris scratched his head and gave me a puzzled look. "Well, yeah, I did, as a matter of fact. Listen, if you didn't do so well, maybe I could help you before the next exam."

I stormed away from him. "No, thanks," I called over my shoulder. "I've had about all the help from you I can take!"

★   ★   ★

When I got to the pool that afternoon, I had the second terrible shock: Coach August had benched me for my poor performance the day before and was letting Jill swim in my place. I rode the bus to the meet in stunned silence. This was the first time in over a year that I wouldn't be competing.

Chris tried his best to console me, but at that moment he was the last person I wanted to listen to. "Coach is just teaching you a lesson," he advised me. "Jill won't swim as well as you can, and you'll still make regionals."

But in the next breath, he was trying to coax me into a midnight meeting.

Anyone who looked closely at me would have been able to tell that my whole life was splitting apart at the seams, but Chris, the guy who said he loved me, was oblivious.

"No how, no way, no time," I told him angrily. "No more Astronomy Club."

At home, in the mailbox, the third terrible shock was waiting for me. It was an envelope addressed, in my father's handwriting, to Miss Amy Wyse. I was afraid to even mention it to Mom, who had a half-hour break between her two jobs and was changing her work clothes. She had sent him a note after I showed her the financial aid form.

I hesitated for a moment before opening it, torn between wanting to know what my father's response to my mother's note was and not wanting any more bad news that day. Finally, nervously, I tore it open and read the first few lines quickly. When I didn't see the phrase "Not on your life!" in the first paragraph, I continued reading, feeling braver and stronger as I got through each line.

Dear Amy, the letter began, in that same crampy script he used to sign my birthday card each year. *Your mom tells me you're planning for college, and of course I want to offer as much help as I can. But things haven't been easy for me these last few years. Did you know that I've changed jobs five times, trying to find something I like?*

When I read the last line, I thought of how Mom had to work two jobs just to make ends meet. I'm sure my father never asked if she liked what she did for a living. "Poor guy," I couldn't help mumbling sarcastically.

"Are you talking to me?" Mom called from her room, giving her hair a last-minute brushing.

"No," I said. "Just talking to myself."

All this by way of saying, I continued to read, *that the contribution I can make toward your tuition isn't much to speak of. But to help with your applications to the state schools* (this, he'd underlined), *I'd like to give you an early graduation present: any electric typewriter of your choice (within reason, of course).*

The last line was so awful that it was almost

funny. I mean, what century was this man living in, anyway? I had been using a word processor ever since I learned to type. I crumpled his letter, walked into the kitchen, and threw it into the trash.

"I see you found your father's letter," Mom said.

"You read it?" I asked.

"I didn't have to," she said, coming over to put her arm around me. "I know your father well enough to know he'll never change. I thought it'd be better if we just got that hope out of the way."

Mom was being so sympathetic that I wanted to burst into tears. "Cheer up, Amy," she said when she saw my eyes welling up. "We'll work things out. The best years of your life are still ahead of you."

I knew that her idea of "working things out" was my applying to a state school. We couldn't afford tuition, let alone room and board, at a private school. I was afraid that if I said that's what I wanted, Mom would go out and get a *third* job.

I wiped the tears from my eyes with the back of my hand and walked with my mom to the driveway. After I watched her drive off down the street, I went back into the empty apartment and strode purposefully to my room.

After the awful day I'd had, what I needed was to write an *A+* project for Ms. Hutchinson and, for once, get a good night's sleep.

*   *   *

148

That night, I spent almost four hours composing a can-you-top-this paper on intimacy. I printed it out on bond paper and placed it in a crisp red folder I found in my desk. After I'd finished, I was feeling relieved and also pretty pleased with myself.

When I heard the tap on my window, my heart didn't leap. It sank. Mom would be home from El Rancho any minute. Technically, I was still grounded, and by that time—ten fifteen—I was supposed to be fast asleep.

I opened the window and glared at Chris. "What are you doing here?" I asked him. "I told you, no more."

"Please, Amy. It's still early, and I won't keep you up late," he promised. Something reckless in his eyes alarmed me. What if he did something stupid, I worried, like hang around until Mom pulled into the driveway and we were both caught? That's when I decided that getting him safely out of there would be easier if I just played along.

I glanced at my glow-in-the-dark alarm clock and saw that there wasn't time to change back into my clothes. "Stay right there. I'll come outside."

There was really no graceful way to climb out my window wearing an ankle-length nightgown. "Let me help you," Chris said as I balanced, half in and half out of the window. I rested my arms on his strong swimmer's shoulders, and he lifted me in his arms and carried me to the lawn.

I shivered as he set me down in the shadow of the oleanders, where we could stay out of sight. "Cold?" Chris asked. I nodded, and he pulled me close.

Around us, it had started to thunder. In the distance, I saw a flash of lightning.

"I can't stay," I told him. "It's going to pour. Besides, my mom will be home any minute."

"Stay just a little while," Chris begged.

"I can't risk it," I told him. "By the time my mom gets home from work, I've got to be back inside, asleep in my bed."

Just then, the skies broke open, and the rain came down in torrents. "Chris, I can't—" I started to protest, but he had already taken my hand and was pulling me to the shelter of a palm tree. Its fronds made a puny umbrella.

"Amy," he said, pulling me closer, "I had to tell you. When you were mad at me today, I realized . . ." He paused for a moment, as if unsure of his words. "It's just that I love you. I don't want you to be angry. I don't want to be apart."

It was exciting to hear those words, but it was a little scary too. I wasn't sure I was ready.

"Well, we have to have *some* time apart," I tried to joke. "You know—to see our families, change our clothes." But Chris wasn't laughing, and he held me so tightly I could hear his heart beating in his chest.

150

"Chris, I really have to go," I told him, pulling away.

"Amy, you know I'd do anything for you," Chris whispered.

I stared at him for a moment as he held my arm, and I realized that though he meant what he said, it wasn't true. If it were he wouldn't be holding me so tight when I was desperate to get back to the safety of my bedroom.

"Chris, listen," I said, getting anxious. "If my mom comes home and I'm out here soaking wet in my bathrobe, we're both going to be in big trouble. Don't you even care?"

"Of course I care," Chris said.

"Then let me go," I protested. "If you really care, you'll do what's best for me. All these late nights don't even seem to affect you. You work half as hard as I do and end up with much better grades. You swim as well as ever, and I end up getting benched. You may not need the space, but I do!"

Just then, a pair of headlights flashed across the front lawn as a car turned into our drive. "Quick! Duck!" I said, pushing Chris into the oleanders. I recognized the whiny sound of the car's engine. I didn't even have to look to know that it was Mom.

"You've got to get out of here!" I whispered, and without waiting for an answer, I took off for my open window. I prayed that Mom would fumble with her door keys, giving me a few extra seconds to get inside.

"I'll wait for you," Chris promised, running beside me.

"Don't you dare!" I snapped at him. "If my mother catches you here, I'll be grounded for the rest of my life."

"It's not a crime for us to want to be together," Chris said defiantly as he helped me back through the window.

I couldn't believe he was talking in such a loud voice when my mom was just fifty feet away, probably turning her key in the lock. "Go home!" I whispered desperately. "Go home and leave me alone! I mean it!"

Chris started to protest, but I slid the window shut. Then I crawled into bed and pulled up the covers just as Mom cracked open my door to check in on me. My heart was pounding, and I was relieved when she closed the door.

As I lay there in bed, tears ran down my face. I didn't want to give up Chris, I really didn't.

But I couldn't take sneaking around behind my mother's back anymore, I couldn't take feeling tired all the time, I couldn't take feeling so distant from Blythe and Rick, and I couldn't take failure in school and on the swim team.

If this is what being in love meant, then maybe my mom was right: I wasn't meant to be in love.

Chapter Fifteen

FOR THE NEXT week at school, I stayed as far from Chris as possible. It was hard, and I missed him constantly, but I had finally admitted to myself that being in love and achieving my goals just didn't mix. The only way I was going to get back on track was by giving him up.

Blythe was great—she had totally forgiven me for yelling at her about the dance. Every day she waited with me and kept me occupied until Chris had left the classroom after physics, and at swimming I made sure to stay in the locker room until Coach August blew his whistle for practice.

I really concentrated on my swimming. Often, I stayed after practice to get some extra swimming in. To be completely honest, part of my swimming late had to do with avoiding Chris. But mostly I wanted to prove to Coach August, and to myself, that I was prepared for the regionals.

One night I had a really bizarre dream. Chris and I were at the regionals, but I was swimming his breaststroke events instead of my freestyle, and he wasn't swimming at all. He had come to compete as a diver. He turned tight somersaults high in the air and then sliced the water cleanly just a few feet from where I was swimming laps in the pool.

The water, however, was not clear and sparkling blue, but a sinister, murky, river brown. When he landed, it creepily closed up around his body, like a sea anemone. Dirty bubbles rose to the surface while the audience applauded.

In the middle of the race, I stopped swimming and dog-paddled to the place where he'd entered the water, afraid that he might drown. But then I heard his voice calling from the pool deck, and I knew that he'd found his way out. I woke up frog-kicking the covers, panicked because I had given up the competition and gotten myself lost.

I told Mom about it that morning at breakfast. She seemed to think it was a pretty easy dream to interpret. "Amy, you're drowning in all the pressure you've put yourself under," she said.

I stared at her in disbelief, anger rising in my throat. "Who are you to talk about pressure?" I demanded angrily. "You're the one who's always pressuring me to get good grades and win a swimming scholarship so I can go to college." I was really steamed. "You don't want me to have any kind of life. You won't even let me date!"

I was amazed by the rage in my own voice, but I couldn't stop myself. The floodgates had opened, and there was nothing I could do to close them. "I can't do everything you want me to!" I yelled at her in a choked voice. "I can't get perfect grades! I'm never going to be an Olympic swimmer!"

Suddenly my anger broke and sadness rushed in to replace it. Before I knew it, tears were streaming down my cheeks, and my chest was heaving with quiet sobs. "I can't live your life for you, Mom," I whispered. "I can't make your dreams come true."

Mom's face was anguished, and when she stood up from her chair I was scared she was going to walk out of the kitchen. But she didn't. She came over and put her arms around me and rocked me gently back and forth.

I don't even know how long we stood there in our bathrobes, holding each other. I just knew it felt good to be in her arms and feel like her little girl again.

"I'm sorry, Amy," she said at last when she pulled away. I could tell from the streaks on her face that she'd been crying too. "I only wanted to protect you. I wanted to save you from making the mistakes I've made. But I know I can't. I have to let you grow up."

A fresh wave of tears filled my eyes as she pushed my hair back from my forehead.

"Sometimes it's hard to know the right way to love someone," she said in a soft voice. "It's hard to know when and how to let go."

I realized when she said that, she could have been talking about Chris.

Three days before the junior-senior dance, Rick called and asked me to go with him. As a friend.

"That is, if you're not already going with Shepherd," he said, as if the rumor of our breakup hadn't circulated throughout the entire school.

"I'd love to go to the dance with you," I said truthfully. "There's just one problem—I already have a date."

"You do?" Rick asked. "But I thought you and Shepherd broke up."

"We did," I said, and then I couldn't help laughing. "Blythe doesn't have a date, and she and I agreed to go together."

"How about if Blythe comes with us?" Rick suggested.

"That's a great idea," I told him. "The three-some is back in action. You call her."

He and I talked for a few minutes more, then hung up. I sat by the phone, smiling. Rick wasn't right for me, and I knew it. But he was right for Blythe, only he didn't know it yet. I knew he wasn't seeing beyond her crazy clothes and her outspoken ideas and all their years of platonic friendship, so before I hung up, I spent a few minutes talking up Blythe's romantic side to Rick.

Then I called up Blythe to discuss what we were going to wear to the dance. I knew I couldn't possibly ask Mom for money to buy a dress. As usual, Blythe came to my rescue.

"You can wear something of mine," she said. "I'll be right over to pick you up."

A half hour later Blythe was searching her large closet for something I could borrow. She sorted through a row of worn-once fancy dresses and then pulled out her brand-new black velvet. "This would look great on you," she said.

"Blythe, you haven't even worn that yet," I protested.

"I know." Blythe sighed and smoothed the fabric around the neckline lovingly. "Once I got it home, I decided it just didn't fit."

"Right," I told her, squinting skeptically. "Like you really gained twenty pounds since you bought it." I knew she was pretending it didn't fit because she was trying to make me feel better about having broken up with Chris. I hadn't told her about my conversation with Rick—I was nervous that she'd get mad if she found out I'd been playing match-maker.

"Why don't you try this on again," I said to Blythe, "just to make sure."

While she was dressing, the phone in the hall-way rang. "I'll get it," I said, running. "I'll bet it's for you."

"Who could be calling?" Blythe said sarcasti-cally. "You're already here."

"Hello?" I said, and my suspicions were con-firmed. "Hi. Yeah, hang on just a sec."

I went to Blythe's bedroom door. "It's Rick," I whispered. "And I don't think he wants to talk about PSATs."

"You didn't!" Blythe screamed at me, covering her face so that I couldn't tell if she was angry or pleased. "You didn't actually ask Rick if I could tag along on your date to the dance!"

"Of course not," I said. "I told him I had a date with you and that he could tag along with us."

"I am so embarrassed," Blythe said.

"Blythe, what's the deal?" I demanded. "The three of us have gone to parties and dances together before."

"But that was before . . ."

Blythe's sentence trailed off, but I finished it for her in my head. *Before he kissed me? Before you realized you were falling in love with him?*

"Fine," Blythe said at last. "We'll go. The Awesome Threesome reunited."

I smiled. "Great."

"But"—she pointed a warning finger at me—"don't you dare go acting like it's anything else."

I nodded innocently. "Whatever you say."

So Blythe and I shared a date, and she shared her beautiful peacock-blue silk dress with me. And that's how it happened that on Friday we made our entrance, three abreast, at the junior-senior dance.

Sure, some people were whispering about our strange date. But they'd seen it before, and the way I figured it, I had the best of both worlds: my best friend and my other best friend. I tried not to think of what I was missing without Chris.

I have a picture of us from that night, taken by one of those cheesy freelance photographers with the ruffled shirt and sly smile. The three of us are laughing hysterically, posing against this odd Hawaiian backdrop of plastic potted plants. Rick appears more relaxed and happy than I've ever seen him. Blythe is in the middle, getting Rick's attention by making a face. I'm off to one side, looking out toward the dance floor, as if I'm searching for something I've lost.

"Come on!" Blythe said after the picture was taken and our threesome recorded for posterity. "Let's get out there and show the school that this trio knows how to dance!"

159

The first song didn't go so well, though. I love to dance, but it was so crowded on the dance floor that my arms were practically pinned to my sides and I could barely move my hips. Besides, I felt self-conscious, especially since Rick was moving so carefully, swaying a half inch in either direction and stiffly snapping his fingers. It was about as much fun as one of those dances in junior high, where the girls are dancing together, while the boys huddle together against the cafeteria wall.

Blythe circled around us making fun of our serious expressions, doing her best to get us both to loosen up. Then, in a fit of desperation, she tried another tactic. Blythe, who can be very persuasive, convinced a whole group of kids to get in a long line and do the Bunny Hop.

I was shocked that Rick joined in immediately, grabbing Blythe by the waist and following her down some imaginary trail. "What a nutcase!" he said appreciatively, as I hooked on the line. Blythe's idea had been risky—I mean, the Bunny Hop's not exactly the picture of cool. But as always, she knew just the right thing to make people laugh and have a good time. Even Rick was moving easier, and I could tell by his face that he was greatly relieved. The line got longer and longer, and soon half the students had joined in, weaving all around the gym.

"I'm thirsty," I finally told Rick, hopping in my

bare feet right out of the bunny line. "I'm going to get something to drink."

"I'll come with you," Rick said. He broke off from Blythe's waist regretfully, but I took his hands in mine and reattached them to her.

"Stay here, have fun," I told him. "I'm fine."

I made my way across the dance floor, dodging spinning bodies and flailing limbs. Finally, I found a table in the corner where I could listen to the music and watch Blythe and Rick have fun . . . and search the room for Chris's face.

I knew there was very little chance he would actually come, so when I first saw his face across the dark, crowded gym, I thought I was imagining it.

But when he returned my gaze I knew it was really him. I felt my stomach drop and my pulse quicken. He hadn't bothered to improve on his usual outfit of jeans and a T-shirt, but he looked heartbreakingly gorgeous anyway.

He stared at me intensely, and I felt a flush warm my cheeks. I knew the silk dress made me look much more glamorous than I usually did.

He stared at me, and I stared back at him. Part of me was dying to go over and talk to him, to ask him to dance to a slow song. The feeling of missing him was almost like a physical pain.

When the first few notes of a slow song started, I resolved to go over to him. I was barely out of my seat when I saw another girl approach him. I immediately recognized her as Heather Gray, a senior who used to come cheer for him at swim meets last year.

Heather whispered something in his ear. Chris gave me a long questioning look before he stood up and followed her onto the dance floor.

Rick and Blythe and I left a little while after that. I couldn't stand the idea of staying. The two of them dropped me off at home. To be honest, it was a little depressing. In addition to missing Chris, my threesome was now a twosome and a onesome. Maybe I had done *too* good a job as matchmaker, I thought. I wanted Rick and Blythe to be together, but I felt a little left out.

"Talk to you," Blythe called, waving cheerfully, as the two of them drove away.

I was happy for her, but I missed the way we usually talked afterward, going over every detail of any party or dance.

I let myself into the quiet apartment, where Mom had already gone to bed. She'd left a note on my dresser. "Sweetie, I hope you had a great time." The note lay on top of the key Chris had given me, and for some reason, the sight made me feel so lonely I started to cry. I opened a drawer, threw the key inside, and slammed the drawer shut as hard as I could.

Chapter Sixteen

THERE'S A TRADITION in Phoenix: every other
year or so we get what the weather forecast-
ers call the "Five-Hundred-Year Flood." It starts
with a rain shower that lingers for a few days, then
it turns into a torrent when the days string together
into weeks. Since the desert's too hard and dry to
make use of this big gulp of water, whatever falls
from the sky rushes ankle-deep through the valley,
stalling cars and ebbing like a muddy ocean onto
people's front lawns.

Usually, the rain doesn't arrive until late in
December, but that year it got a running start. For
days before regionals it poured relentlessly.

When the Dolphins set out on Saturday for the
two-hour trek to Tucson, huge rainwater lakes cov-
ered the desert, looking as unbelievable as a mirage.

"This must be what it looks like on the moon," I said to Cheryl Wagner, a senior who was sitting next to me on the bus. Chris, seated a row ahead, turned around and smiled at me appreciatively. "I don't know why we have to drive all the way to Tucson," he joked. "We could just park at one of these pools and hold the meet right here."

My heart started thumping. It was one of those almost-moments, where one of us could have apologized. But after an awkward, tension-filled silence, we both turned back to our windows, and we didn't speak again until after the meet.

Regionals were like a Who's Who of worthy opponents: names I recognized from the roster as state record holders and faces I'd seen many times before at the starting block. Looking around at the teams represented, I tried to think of the regionals as just another practice meet. All that talent and pressure could be pretty intimidating. If you weren't careful, it could really psych you out. Especially considering there were coaches from at least a dozen colleges scouting there. Especially considering my mom had taken an afternoon off from the bank to watch me swim.

I wasn't surprised to find Jill in the locker room a half hour before meet time, her eyes red-rimmed from holding back tears. At first, I just talked to some of my other teammates and pretended not to notice, figuring she was just burned because Coach August had noticed my improved flip turn and steadily improving times, and had chosen me for the 100-free. But finally, I had to say something. The most important meet of the season was just about to start, and she didn't even have her suit on.

I sat down next to her on the bench and bent down to untie my shoes. "Something wrong?" I said casually, and Jill burst out crying.

"I can't get into the pool," she said.

"Sure you can," I told her. "Every team is allowed a fifteen-minute warm-up."

"You don't get it," she said. "I can't get into the pool."

"What do you mean?"

"When I think about swimming, I feel like I'm going to choke," she said, holding her throat. "My parents are out there, and they expect me to win."

At first, I thought Jill was just being dramatic, maybe as a sneaky way of psyching me out. But the scared look on her face told me she was serious. There was no time for speculation, or for old rivalries. "Close your eyes," I told her, and amazingly, she did. "Breathe deeply. Now, picture yourself swimming, and say 'STOP!' out loud if you see yourself starting to choke."

I got her to change into her suit, and then I sat there with her again, coaching, until a few minutes before the meet. "You can do it, Renfrew," I said,

165

as she took her place, tensed her leg muscles, straightened her shoulders, and summoned her courage to swim. Jill smiled weakly in my direction, but Shannon, who was standing nearby, looked at me like I was nuts.

"Since when are you two friends?" she asked, disbelieving.

I turned and saw Jill's parents in the bleachers, and I felt as though I finally understood where she was coming from. The two sat stiffly together, frowning intensely, as though their will alone could make their daughter win.

I quickly scanned the crowded bleachers for my mom, my own source of pressure and expectation. When she saw me look up, she waved and smiled. I waved and smiled back.

"Jill needed help," I said to Shannon. "After this meet, who knows? We may never be friends again."

When Jill hit the water humming with speed, I couldn't have been prouder if she were my own prodigy. "Good going," Coach August whispered to me as Jill turned on her last lap, and I smiled. Not only had I maybe made a friend that day, but I'd discovered a new kind of visualization. I'd been so wrapped up in Jill's performance that I'd forgotten to be nervous about my opponents, the hope of a swimming scholarship, and my own mom's presence.

* * *

166

As it turned out, the freestyle I swam that day at regionals was my personal best. I made three near-perfect flip turns and beat my previous best by more than three seconds. Not only that, I won the race.

Practically every muscle in my body was trembling with exhaustion and excitement as I hoisted myself out of the water. "I felt like I was flying," I told my mom when she rushed down to hug me afterward.

"You were wonderful, Amy! I'm so proud of you," she exclaimed. Then a momentary look of uncertainty passed over her face. "Not that I wouldn't have been just as happy with a second-place finish."

I laughed and hugged her again before she went back to the bleachers to retrieve her stuff. At least she was trying.

Rick came up to me next. He was there to interview the team for the *Thunder*. "The longer I swam, the more energy I had," I told him. "It was almost as if time were moving backward, the way it would in a black hole."

"If that were literally true," Rick couldn't resist adding, scribbling down the quote, "then right about now, you'd be ready to explode."

"Lucky for Amy," said Blythe, hurrying over to us with her camera, "she's not as literal-minded as you are, Finnegan."

"Someone's got to hold this paper to its standards," Rick said with a laugh, and the two rolled their eyes in unison.

I grabbed the camera from Blythe's hands and took a picture of them. I couldn't resist.

"Caption: Record-breaking Swimmer Photographs Lowly Reporters," Blythe said.

Framing Blythe and Rick in the camera's viewfinder, I could see what a perfect couple they made—both blond, both good-looking, and both holding notepads and pens.

"What's this?" Chris asked, wandering over and tossing down his gym bag. "Now you're moonlighting as the *Thunder*'s photographer?"

My heart leapt. "I thought the reporters might give me the scoop on how you did," I told him shyly.

When Chris swam his events, I'd been busy coaching Jill through her panic attack, so Rick's dramatic description for the *Thunder* would have to suffice. "Shepherd swam with new determination," Rick read from his notepad, "charting his best-ever time in the breaststroke, inspired by a mysterious source."

"It's not so mysterious," Chris corrected him. "I've always been a fast swimmer, but Amy helped me to see that I really wanted to win."

I looked up at him and gave him a huge smile.

"Oooh, great photo," Blythe cried out, rushing to take our picture.

"Finnegan, your face is mighty pretty, but we don't want it in this shot," she said. "Lean back toward me so I can get these photos taken and send these poor, tired Dolphins home."

"One more question," Rick requested, as Chris and I began to walk away. "Now that you've done so well at regionals, what's ahead for both of you?"

Chris turned to me then, his eyes apologetic but full of pride too. "From now on," he said, "I'm going to work on setting some new goals—and not just in the pool."

Rick stopped writing for a moment. "Isn't it a bit late in the season for 'setting new goals'?" he asked.

"It's never too late if you're passionate enough," Chris answered without missing a beat.

"What about you, Amy?" Blythe broke in. I was so busy absorbing Chris's words, I hardly heard her.

I swallowed hard. "I'm hoping to be offered a swimming scholarship at A.S.U.," I said, not wanting to mention my hopes of getting into a smaller, more prestigious university. "I've still got next year to reach that goal. And in the meantime, I'm going to figure out a way to accomplish my goals and have a life too." I looked at Chris and our eyes locked. "I think I've got enough passion for both," I said.

My mom was standing by the door to the locker

room as Chris and I approached. I suddenly felt nervous. Would she acknowledge him? Would she say anything? There were a few awkward moments of silence before my mom reached out and shook his hand.

"Congratulations, Chris," she said warmly. "You're a really impressive swimmer."

Chris looked surprised and pleased. "Thank you, Mrs. Turner."

She gave him a smile before she turned away.

I felt a flood of relief. My mom really was trying.

Chapter Seventeen

T HAT NIGHT, MOM threw me a surprise party in honor of my victory at regionals. She'd invited Blythe and Rick and served every food I'd loved since childhood: mashed potatoes, pizza, cornbread, chimichangas, macaroni and cheese, and pecan pie.

"What? No vegetables?" I laughed when I saw the weird spread.

"Don't mashed potatoes count?" Blythe asked.

Mom had also strung a banner reading "Congratulations!" across the dining area. The glittering foil letters connected like a row of paper dolls.

I loved being a guest in my own house, and I'm sure I ate twice as much as everyone else. It was fun listening to Blythe and Rick talk excitedly about the *Thunder*, especially since I felt responsible for bringing them together. But seeing them as a couple reminded me of Chris, and I missed him.

Even though I was sure I missed him, I wasn't sure I wanted us to get back together. I couldn't let myself get so wrapped up in him that I'd forget everything else that was important to me. I didn't want to lose myself again.

"I propose a toast to Amy," Mom said, bringing me back to reality. She carried the pecan pie to the table. We all raised our ginger ale glasses.

"To her success, her happiness . . ." Mom's voice wobbled a little with emotion. "And her growing up."

I smiled at her as we clinked glasses.

"And may she swim the fins off everybody at the state competition," Mom couldn't resist adding.

Two days later at school, I got some really good news. I learned that I'd done much better than I thought I would on the PSATs. In fact, I'd made the semifinalists for the National Merit Scholarships. At lunchtime, I called my mom at work, and she was as happy as I was. Rick and Blythe also did well, so we shared a group hug and a burrito grande at lunchtime.

But the person I really wanted to share my happiness with wasn't there. Chris had missed school for the past two days.

I couldn't help wondering where he was, hoping he wasn't sick, and wishing I could see him.

That night after my mom had gone to bed, I pulled the ladder from the oleanders and leaned it against the wall of the apartment building as Chris and I had done together on so many nights. I slowly climbed up to the roof, thinking about the times he would grab my feet, pretend to shake the ladder, put his hands on my waist, kiss my neck.

When I got up there I lay back on the tiles and gazed up at the night sky. It was a perfect night for stargazing. But I could only think of Chris's face and all the kisses we had shared. As proud as I was of my accomplishments in the last few weeks, I wanted so badly to share my happiness with him.

At first I heard a rustling in the hedges. Then a creaking noise. My heart was pounding when I saw a shadowy form appear on the roof. Whether it was pounding out of fear or hope, I'm not sure.

I felt an incredible rush of joy as Chris's face came into view. I held out my arms to him, and he pulled me against his chest in a breathtaking, knee-weakening hug.

"Congratulations!" he said as he held me. "I just heard your good news."

I drew apart from him. "How did you know?"

"How could I not know," Chris laughed, "with the test-score network circulating the news?"

"Come on, Chris," I said doubtfully. "You don't care about those things anyway."

He looked at me for a long time before he answered. "I do care about them if they make you happy," he said.

And that's when I realized that maybe he did understand what had gone wrong between us.

As he sat down beside me and gently draped his arm over my shoulder, a feeling of hope expanded in my chest. There was so much I wanted to tell him and ask him that I could hardly speak. "Chris, where have you been?" was the first thing that came out.

"Amy, I've missed you so much," he said in a rush. "There are so many things I want to tell you. I meant it the other day when I said I wanted to set new goals. One of them was taking my college applications more seriously. I've spent the last two days visiting Stanford."

"You're kidding me," I said, my eyes widening in surprise.

Chris shook his head. "I'd gotten the catalog, and I was worried it was the kind of place where you had to be pre-med or pre-law, or at least declare your major on your first day. But when I visited, I met some really cool people. The guy I roomed with is a sophomore, and he's taken courses in practically every department in the school. In the summers he builds houses for low-

174

income families for Habitat for Humanity, which is exactly what I did this summer."

"That's wonderful," I said. "You could take art courses"—I was thinking of the sketch he had done of me—"or ecology?"

"Yep," Chris said. "I liked Stanford so much, I've decided to apply early-decision."

I was glad Chris was so excited. After all, it was what I'd wanted, wasn't it? For him to take life more seriously. For both of us to be involved in things besides each other.

But another part of me was disappointed that he would be so far away, and that he could leave me behind so easily. "That's really wonderful," I said, trying to sound as glad for him as I could.

Chris took my hand and squeezed it. "I clocked it—ten hours on the highway between Palo Alto and Phoenix," he said.

"And you know, Stanford has a great swimming program. Their coach will be scouting at the state competition." His face was shy but full of excitement. "I think you'd love Stanford as much as I did, Amy. And if you do qualify for the National Merit Scholarship—"

"Whoa." I put my hand up and laughed. "I think you're letting your imagination get away from you here." I was laughing, but the truth was that the idea sounded incredible and exciting and wonderful to me. If there was any way I could go to

175

Stanford, I promised myself I would try.

"I know you can do it, Amy. And we still have the rest of this year and a whole summer for meetings of the Astronomy Club." My smile faded at that moment. If Chris and I were going to be together, there were still some things that needed to be said. I took a deep breath. "Chris, I want to see you, but I can't keep meeting you at midnight, then getting up for classes the next day. I want you in my life, but I won't be happy if I can't keep my grades up and swim well and—"

"I know," he said quickly. "I've been selfish, and I know it. I wanted to spend every minute with you, and that's not good for either of us." He looked at me long and hard, with such tenderness that I felt a tingle travel the length of my body. "I'm ready to start all over if you are," he said.

I took his hand again. "So . . . no more sneaking around?"

He nodded solemnly.

"And no more midnight visits to my window?"

Chris made a face, but nodded.

"And when we study together, we really study?"

He nodded again.

"And when we swim together we put on our bathing suits first?"

A rueful smile crept onto Chris's face as he nodded again.

"Maybe we could try going to the movies or to

dinner," he suggested. "You know, things people do on ordinary dates."

And then we shared another smile, because we both knew that nothing we did together would ever be ordinary.

"Here's to the end of the Astronomy Club," he said. He leaned forward and took my face in both his hands. "And the beginning of true love."

When his lips met mine, I felt a rush of happiness that took my breath away. It was a kiss filled with promises. And with hope.

We hope you enjoyed reading this book. If you would like to receive further information about available titles in the Bantam series, just write to the address below, with your name and address:

KIM PRIOR
Bantam Books
61–63 Uxbridge Road
London W5 5SA

If you live in Australia or New Zealand and would like more information about the series, please write to:

SALLY PORTER
Transworld Publishers (Australia) Pty Ltd
15–25 Helles Avenue
Moorebank
NSW 2170
AUSTRALIA

KIRI MARTIN
Transworld Publishers (NZ) Ltd
3 William Pickering Drive
Albany
Auckland
NEW ZEALAND

All Transworld titles are available by post from:-
Bookservice by Post
PO Box 29
Douglas
Isle of Man
IM99 1BQ

Credit Cards accepted. Please telephone 01624 675137
or fax 01624 670923

Please allow £0.75 per book for post and packing UK.
Overseeas customers allow £1.00 per book for post and packing.

Sweet Dreams are fresh, fun and exciting – alive with the flavour of the contemporary teen scene – the joy and doubt of *first love*. *Your* kind of stories, written about people like *you*!

Recent Bantam titles in the Sweet Dreams series. Ask your bookseller for the titles you have missed:

SWEET VALLEY HIGH™

The top-selling teenage series starring identical twins Jessica and Elizabeth Wakefield and all their friends at Sweet Valley High. One new title every month!

SWEET VALLEY HIGH™

created by Francine Pascal

Join Elizabeth, Jessica and their friends from Sweet Valley on their wildest adventures ever – at Sweet Valley University.